STRANDED
ON
GRZBT

Far Stars Universe

Book 1

Melisse Aires

BLURB

Scifi Romance with love, Passion, Adventure and No Gore!

Abducted from Wichita by gross, stinky space worms, three women and a teenager spend months in a cage, their only friend a tiny trunk-nosed alien animal, Velvet.

Unexpectedly freed from captivity by a dock accident, the four have to find a way to survive on a busy space dock. They don't know the language, have no one to help them, and don't know how long they can stay in the small spaceship. Slavers might kidnap them at any time. But they know things are always better with a little money.

Mimi has the great idea to busk for alien money cubes. They work on a few common Christmas Carols, devise costumes, and head to a large, alien city.

Kyre Valryssian accompanies his family to an outdoor restaurant on the resort planet Fera. To their shock, they hear their private family language, English, sung by women in the park! Bridge Officer Kyre must investigate, because Earth is not a planet with interstellar travel.

The Far Stars Universe:

Lighthearted scifi romance set in a universe of many aliens, reminiscent of a certain bar scene in a popular movie from my youth.

CONTENTS

ACKNOWLEDGMENTS

Cover Artist: Melisse Aires
Stock Photos:
Pixabay.com
Depositphotos Stock Photos
Canstock Photos

Editor: Dave Ellis

CHAPTER ONE

Mimi woke on a hard metal floor, shoulders and back aching. A rancid, putrid odor rushed into her nose, making her gag. It wiped out any drowsiness. "What is that stench?" It was like sewer mixed with rotten meat. She leaped up with a groan, only to bang her head on heavy wire and fall on her butt.

She sat in a cage made of thick wire welded to the metal floor. Two other women were awake, staring outside the cage, not acknowledging her. A Goth teen girl sprawled unconscious on the floor.

"Wha...?" Mimi looked where the other two were staring. Four puke green worms, with belts around their middles, sat on a bench in front of some type of computer. A small round screen showed a black background with pricks of light.

One of the women looked at her and pointed to the worms. "That's where the smell comes from." The speaker was a few years older than Mimi, who was twenty-four. She wore a pink and gray seersucker dress with a pink sweater. The gray flats looked far too orthopedic for a woman in her late twenties or early thirties. Her dark curly hair was falling out of a French twist.

The other woman, with long blonde hair in a braid, wore a denim jumper. She didn't move or acknowledge she'd noticed Mimi waking.

"I don't think she's well," the dark-haired woman said with a small sob. "She hasn't said a word since she woke."

Their clothes gave Mimi a clue they were from the neighborhood church on her block. "I don't remember anything."

The woman nodded. "You'll remember pretty soon. They shot us with some kind of ray," she said and then sat silently. The blonde woman looked like she'd had a psychotic break, just staring. The teen slept on.

Mimi closed her eyes. Maybe this was all a nightmare, and she'd wake in her normal bed. She sagged against the stiff wire of the cage and closed her eyes.

***

Memory returned in a rush—

Mimi sprinted from her car toward her apartment, glad she had gotten off work at the Perky Perk early. She had an assignment due tomorrow. Church people were just driving off from their evening activities. A Goth teen whizzed by her on a scooter, black clothes flapping.

A flash of light and two green worms stood under the streetlight near the church parking lot. They wore tool belts and one pointed a tube right at two modestly clad ladies walking down the church steps. A pink beam shot out of a tube and swept across two church ladies.

The women disappeared.

What? Mimi gaped at the empty space in disbelief.

Then a worm swept the pink beam toward her.

All went black.

***

"Is that space?" Mimi asked the dark-haired woman. "In the circle screen? Did we get abducted by aliens? You think we are on a spaceship?" She knew she was babbling, but she didn't care.

The dark-haired woman nodded. "There's a bathroom, sort of, if you climb through that hole in the cage." A hole in the cage lined up with a crudely cut hole in the metal wall. "The water's hot. I'm Acacia, she's Hannah."

"Mimi." She crawled through the hole to a dimly lit square room. One wall might be a door, but she couldn't see how to open it. Two stools with dark openings stood against the far wall. Water dripped from a tube in the ceiling. A metal drain covered with a grate filled the floor. Green scum grew on the metal of the grate.

Everything had an unpleasant odor, like an outdoor toilet.

"I thought aliens were supposed to be advanced," she grumbled when she crawled back to the cage.

"These might be your less-advanced type of alien," said Acacia. "They keep smacking the console with a wrench thing."

"I remember the worms now. They had a ray tube. I watched them aim at you, and you two disappeared."

The brunette sniffed and nodded her head toward the blonde. "We were leaving choir practice."

"Okay. I'm sure this is a huge shock. This other girl is still knocked out?"

Acacia nodded her head. "She's just a kid, so maybe it affected her more? She probably doesn't weigh very much."

***

The first few days Mimi watched the aliens constantly from the cage. They all did. She was twitchy and found it hard to sleep, even though she was exhausted.

Hannah stared, the teen girl Chloe glared, and Acacia tried to help them, even though there was no help to give.

Sometimes all the lights went off, which was probably bad. A worm gave the console a good whack with a metal tool, turning the lights back on. Some electrical problem, Mimi thought. *If spaceships have wires and stuff. Maybe they don't know how to fix it.*

Scary.

"They don't seem too bright. Or they don't really know how to fly this spaceship," Mimi said to Acacia.

"I think it is a bucket-of-bolts type spaceship," Acacia said. "Dented walls. Is that white stuff in that hole insulation? Scorch marks. Some computer buttons look melted."

"Looks like they had a leak over there," Mimi pointed to some dull yellow stains on the metal wall.

Hannah finally started talking. Mimi often longed for the time when she was too shocked to talk.

Hannah was strident.

I should give her a break. We were abducted by space worms. No one is at their best.

Hannah thought the worms had a substance abuse issue. "We've seen them snorting a gray powder!" she said in her bossy voice.

"I think that is how they eat. Maybe it's soil, since they look like earthworms with little hairy arms," Mimi said. "But who knows? They're aliens!"

"Alien centipedes with bad BO," Chloe the teen grumbled.

We aren't adjusting well, Mimi thought several days later. She had no idea how to help them all to get along. What do you do, stuck in a cage?

Chloe growled instead of speaking most of the time. That kid was seriously depressed.

"They probably plan to lay eggs in us. Live food for their larva," Chloe popped up one night after the second kibble feeding, when they normally went to sleep. "You know some bugs do that."

"H-How can you say that?" Hannah stared at her. Chloe laughed hysterically.

Hannah yelled, "You need to shut your mouth and quit being such a pain!" She wagged a finger in Chloe's face, "Listen and obey!"

Chloe giggled. "Make me."

Mimi knew she just enjoyed winding Hannah up. Mimi wanted to do the same sometimes, but she restrained herself.

Chloe giggle louder, rolling on the floor. "Not in your Sunday school, Ma'am."

"This has to stop," Mimi hollered at Hannah and Chloe. "Chloe, don't try to make things worse. We all know something worse might be coming. We're all scared and helpless."

She turned to Hannah. "Your church is back on Earth, and we're not following you just because you're the pastor's daughter. We haven't voted you in as boss. Plus, I've seen you bully Acacia and that stops now."

She hugged Acacia and Chloe. "Chloe's only fourteen. Give her a damn break."

Actually, Mimi thought Chloe was more like twelve, the little liar. They had showered (well, water dripped, no one could call that a shower) together at first, buddy system. She was a complete little girl. Some girls looked all grown up at fourteen. Not Chloe. No signs of puberty.

Mimi glared at Hannah. She got more annoyed with her every day, and had to talk herself down from confrontations all the time.

"We need to stick together," Acacia said. "I know this is horrible, with the cage, and that gross bathroom. And the worms stink so bad! But we need to try and get along."

Mimi sighed. "You're right. Sorry," she mumbled.

Acacia was the oldest, a plump, kindhearted, thirty-one-year-old. She seemed naive to Mimi in some ways, but in others she had a wisdom for helping. She'd been a church secretary since she was eighteen, and lived at home with her grandparents.

Hannah was close to thirty, and actually beautiful, with long fine blonde hair and big blue eyes. She worked in a bank and ran half of the church.

Mimi, an accounting major with a theater minor, was working her way through college. She was thin but had a few curves thanks to a small waist. Her hair was super short since classes, theater practice, and work gave her no time to fix her hair.

Chloe said she was fourteen and in the ninth grade. She would be gorgeous one day, Mimi thought. Dark hair, golden skin, hazel eyes, dimples when she ever smiled, tall and rail thin.

She got right in Hannah's face. "But Acacia giving you half her dog food? That stops now. In fact, you're going to be paying Acacia back those kibbles."

The four were fed some type of dry, brown, tasteless chunks.

"Oh, Mimi, we're all on edge," Acacia said in her soft voice. "It's all right, really."

"Still, she gets no more of your food. That is just not right. You need to stand up to her."

Acacia nodded, not looking at Mimi.

"Yeah!" Chloe said in solidarity, giving a fierce look. It actually looked more like a toddler pouting, with her little baby face. Since all her black eye makeup wore off, she looked like a kid.

Hannah backed down and refused to speak to any of the others for days. But when the kibble cups were shoved into the cage, she didn't approach chubby Acacia for any.

The cage was sturdy, made of heavy wire and metal posts welded to the floor. It was only about four foot high, so none of the four could stand up.

Mimi hoped for a while that the bathroom door would be left unlocked. Though, what plan did she have if they got out of the cage? None of them could fly the spaceship back to Earth.

The captors were surprisingly strong, moving cargo boxes to the walls and securing them with nets. Mimi guessed their worm bodies were all muscle. They didn't harass the women, ignored them, actually, and gave each a cup of kibble twice a day.

The worms slept on the bench at the console, rolled up like roly-poly bugs. They never cleaned up their stinky brown ooze, just let it dry.

Days went by, they counted thirteen. Acacia stopped crying, Hannah was as nasty as ever, Chloe liked to drum her fingers on the metal floor and make them all crazy. She called in 'playing drums.'

They played **I Spy** now and then. Mimi and Acacia tried to guess what the things on the console did, and what the worms were talking about with their hoots and screams. Chloe amused them with made up dialog for the hoots. "I'm the stinkiest of allll!"

In the bathroom one day, Mimi took her time under the water drip, washing out her clothes. The worms were asleep.

A flicker of motion caught her eye.

A tiny animal with green and purple fuzz was eating the scum on the grate.

It was actually kind of cute. Plush, silvery sage-green hair, a mousy six-legged body, and a long trunk, like a tiny elephant. On top of its head was a clump of green bristles tipped in purple. Three black button eyes, the center eye larger, looked up at her.

"Hi little guy. Aren't you cute? Are you friendly?"

Mimi had put on just her green work shirt, the rest of her clothes were wet. In the pocket, which had her nametag still attached, were a few kibbles. She crunched one up with her fingernails and slowly sprinkled the kibble bits on the damp grating near the little animal.

It withdrew quickly into the drain. Mimi stayed quiet. Soon the tiny trunk came out and vacuumed up the kibble.

Mimi grinned. Maybe she could make a tiny alien friend.

***

"It might be good to do some exercises," Mimi said. "You know, in case we have a chance to escape."

"Good idea. I was in gymnastics." Chloe was up for it, so they started with crunches, planking, leg lifts and arm circles. Chloe's years of kiddie gymnastics showed.

"We can jog one at a time in the bathroom," Mimi said. "It's probably not healthy for us to sit all the time."

"Crawling all the time is hard on my knees. I'll walk in place in the bathroom," Acacia said.

Hannah was not impressed with the exercise at first. Eventually Acacia persuaded her to join in.

There was nothing else to do. They washed clothes in the bathroom, Hannah led a prayer and Bible verse after morning kibble. **I Spy**, Chloe's humming and drumming, two cups of kibble. That was their day.

Then Acacia's period started. By screaming and stomping, they managed to get the worms' attention, finally.

Maybe Hannah was right and the dust they snorted was a drug. On second thought, nope. Hannah couldn't be right. Mimi gave herself a mental scolding for being so mean. Grumpiness was something they all went through, stuck in the cage.

They showed the worms the bloody underwear after finally getting their attention. What the heck were they supposed to do? Trying to explain human biology to worms was frustrating.

To their surprise, the worms brought a roll of cloth and some type of gel cleaner. They had to tear the cloth with their teeth, but at least it was a solution to the problem.

One by one they all had their periods. The women went through three cycles on the ship, which gave them some sense of time. Three months stuck in a cage. Chloe had her first period at the beginning of the fourth month on the ship. The poor kid had horrible cramps, so Acacia and Mimi took turns sitting with her and rubbing her back.

The gel cleaner was nice, though. They washed their clothes and the entire cage with it. It was a tiny bit less depressing.

The tiny elephant-mouse now knew Mimi.

When the others were napping, Mimi crawled into the bathroom and held several crushed kibbles in her palm. The little beast climbed on, feather light and soft as down. Mimi stroked the velvety fur, and it wiggled in pleasure, showing its belly. It gave tiny trills, like a bird. "Churr-*eet*, Churr-er-er-*eet*." The end of the trill was more like a whistle.

"I'm calling you Velvet," she whispered to it.

Mimi tucked it under her tank top and kept it hidden for a few days. It would siphon water and scum when she was in the bathroom, but then would climb up her pants with tiny, long-fingered paws.

One evening, or at least the time following their second kibble cup, Acacia and Hannah went to sleep. Chloe was watching the worms do things on the console and drumming on her legs.

"Chloe, come here," Mimi whispered. She took Velvet out of her pocket. "Look, I found a pet."

"What the heck!" Chloe whispered, eyes huge. "Well, that's not from Earth."

Acacia woke up and scooted over to them.

"Don't tell Hannah. She's a secret," Mimi said. "I named her Velvet. She's so soft." She offered the little one to the others to pet. Velvet gave her happy purr-whistles.

"How did you find it?" Acacia asked, touching it gently with one finger.

"In the bathroom. It was eating the green stuff."

"How does it eat? I can't see a mouth," Chloe whispered.

"It kind of vacuums with the trunk. See that slit in its trunk? That opens. I crunched up a kibble into powder, and it ate that, too. I almost named her Hoover. But her hair is so soft."

"Don't tell Hannah," Chloe cautioned. "I'm afraid she'll hurt it."

Acacia sighed and gave her a hug. "My lips are sealed. Well, as long as it doesn't bite."

"It won't. I'll keep it under my shirt. I think it likes me."

CHAPTER TWO

"Something's changed," Acacia whispered a few days later. "The worms are crawling all over their instruments."

The worms got frantic as the day went on. The ship jerked and clunked. Bumping into each other, the worms emitted high-pitched screeches in something like panic.

With no seat belts in the cage, the women slid around and bounced. The wire hurt their fingers if they tried to hold on. *Were they crashing?* Mimi thought her heart might pound so hard she would pass out. She braced her legs and held on to Chloe.

Then they came to a stop, with a clunk and a shudder. The worms left the ship through a door they had never noticed before.

"Ahh," Hannah sighed. "The dull whine in the background stopped. Maybe my headache will finally go away."

Chloe, Mimi, and Acacia caught eyes. Hannah had never mentioned headaches in all this time. She rarely spoke at all, unless something sent her into a rant.

"I wonder what's going to happen?" Chloe asked.

"I think they plan to sell us. Or something," Acacia said. "Not anything good."

Every one stared at her. Acacia was normally the cheerful, positive one.

"Well, if they meant to be friendly, they would have tried to get to know us. They stuck us in a cage and ignored us. Like chickens off to the market."

The worms came back, opened the cage, and tied a long rope around each neck, then hooked them together on one leash.

"Don't aliens have high-tech stuff?" Acacia said. "Paralyzing zapper collars?"

"That kind of betrays the fact you don't just watch Bible Church on TV," Mimi said. Acacia shot a guilty glance at Hannah, who huffed. Hannah expounded on the evils of television, books, and movies when the others chatted about movies and shows they had seen. One of the few times she talked to them. Or at them.

"I'm kind of glad it's rope," Chloe piped up. "I can chew through rope. If we can get away to where no one watches us."

Chloe was scary smart for a fourteen-year-old, Mimi thought. "I can see what you mean. Hope we get a chance," Mimi said.

"Did you bring Velvet?" Chloe whispered.

Mimi nodded. "Kibbles, too."

The worms walked them down a metal ramp onto a walkway full of packing crates. The sky was dull and gray.

"A dock," Acacia whispered. The worm's battered ship was held by clamps. "The ship is bigger than I thought it was."

It was tube-shaped with a big round thing at the back. The engine, maybe? Mimi had no idea. There were no other ships shaped like that in their vicinity. There were some large blocky ships and a few classic scifi movie disk-shaped spaceships.

The dock area went on forever, miles. Aliens worked with cranes and truck beds that floated, moving containers. None were human. One looked a little like an elephant with a trunk and two eyes with long eyelashes, and four arms. A few looked a little human, but there was always something different. Oddly pointed skulls, four eyes, bald with cockscomb things on top. Or bony ridged foreheads.

Some were small and had big floppy ears. "Look at all the Dobbys," Chloe whispered.

"This is like the Star Wars Bar scene," Mimi said. Acacia and Chloe nodded.

Some looked nothing like a human. Birdlike legs, big bug eyes. One thing Mimi noticed, they all had some type of hand or appendage that could hold things.

"They all have pincer grips," Acacia said. Again betraying her less-than-pure knowledge of scifi. "Important for manipulating things. Like the worms have all those arms."

Mimi shuddered. The feel of their bristly appendages as the rope was tied on her neck still gave her the creeps.

One of the worms screeched at them and tugged on the rope, turning up a different walkway. Huge warehouses, with large open doors showing more containers, filled their horizon. The worms dragged them into a building. Human-like aliens, except their eyes were on stalks, manned a counter. The worms yelled and the aliens gathered some things.

One by one the aliens shoved each woman into a chair, and harnessed them to keep them from moving. A device came down over the head, so even their heads couldn't move. A needle went in one ear, way in, and another needle went in one eye. It was awful. Horrendous, blinding pain.

When they all had this procedure, they checked on each other. There was no blood.

"The pain is going away. What the heck?" Mimi asked.

"I'm not sure what they did, but I think it might be communication related," said the Scifi Queen. The worms then gave the alien needle guys little cubes.

"I think that's money, the little cubes," Mimi whispered. The worms tied them back up and dragged the women out to the dock area. They continued walking on the main path.

"I'm not hurting anymore," Chloe said after a while.

"Now I'm just worried about where they are taking us," Acacia whispered. They came to an area of larger ships, cruise ship sized. Then something appeared above. Other aliens were looking up at it. Something poked through the gray sky.

"It's not the sky, it's a wall," Mimi said. "A weird wall."

The piece coming though the wall got larger and larger. Workers around them stopped to watch. The worms tried to get them to walk, but the path was full of observers.

"The wall seemed to be made of gel or something soft," Acacia said. "Maybe this isn't a planet after all. Maybe it's a space station."

The gray gel ceiling glommed around the bright white and gold of an enormous ship.

"The ceiling is like ooze, you know, that toy that feels like snot," Chloe said.

The ship was probably twenty times larger than one of the cruise ships. It didn't attempt to pull into a space along the walkway. Instead, it stayed up near the ceiling. A door opened on the side and a flat barge-type ship came out, covered with containers. A covered ship flew out of a different doorway. The barge parked in the docking area. Many workers and hauling machines moved to it and started handling the goods.

A crane-like machine nearby wobbled as it picked up a container.

Velvet, who was riding on Mimi's bra, peeked out at the dock, jumped to her shoulder and climbed up her hair. "Churr-churr-*EET*!"

The whistle was piercing.

"Watch out!" Mimi screamed, as the container began to swing like a pendulum. They all rushed back as far as the rope would let them. One of the worms tried to jerk them forward, rope taut, since they wouldn't move. The four watched the swinging container.

The container broke free of the crane and landed with a boom that shook the ground. They all screamed and covered their faces with their arms. Debris flew everywhere. An alarm blared. Aliens and machines ran around, screeching and howling.

Mimi peeked over her forearm as she covered her face from the flying shards. The container fell right on top of the four worms. The end of the rope fell to the walkway. *We're free!* Mimi grabbed the rope and pulled the others. "Come on!"

The four ran in the chaos of screaming and shouting. Workers came from everywhere. "Quick, we need to get lost in the crates!" Mimi pulled them between two large containers, and they worked through the containers away from the crash site.

"We need to hide somewhere and get this rope off," Acacia said. They walked behind a box and squatted down in the shadows. The rope was knotted, so it was some work to get it undone.

"Let's get away from here," Mimi said once they were separated.

They ran up one aisle and zigzagged through the crates, careful to not be seen. Several minutes later, they came to an area with no one about, no hauling machines or cranes. "N-no cranes. Must b-be a s-storage area," Acacia said, out of breath.

They all sat down to catch their breath. Mimi looked around. "All these crates are broken in some way. Damaged freight. Maybe there's one we can climb inside to hide."

"Or find something we can use." Chloe started looking around. Mimi got up and joined in the search. "Laser guns!"

"We are not stealing guns!" Hannah sounded shocked.

"We were abducted, and now we're on some alien space dock. I personally want to live. If we find something that might help, we should take it." Mimi picked up a piece of broken, sharp fiberglass-like stuff. "This might be handy."

"Are you considering violence?" Hannah said, shocked.

Mimi looked at her. "What kind of fantasy land are you living in? We were being walked with a rope around our necks. No one stopped the worms. All those aliens could see we were wearing clothing. We weren't that different from some of them. Not animals. What do you think the worms had planned for us?"

Hannah was silent.

"Probably a brothel. Or some type of slavery. Manual labor, since none of us can do clerical work here," Acacia said. "I'll help you look."

"Acacia!"

"Hannah, don't even start!" Acacia said tartly. "You know a great deal about Sunday School and Vacation Bible School. But what do you know about surviving on an alien world? You even have a housekeeper at your house, you don't even know how to clean or cook. You're pampered. And you expect people to do what you say."

Hannah stomped off and stood by herself in the shadow of a container.

Acacia, Mimi, and Chloe walked through the containers. Acacia picked up another shard of broken stuff, sharp enough to hurt someone. Hannah followed them some distance away.

"Hey, look at this." Chloe pulled a broken piece off a container. "Clothes, I think." Inside was folded fabric in bright colors, sitting in bins.

Mimi's thoughts raced. "We'll put on some of these clothes, and we'll look different."

"We most certainly will not steal these clothes!" Hannah said, shoving her way up to the container, outraged.

"We're not in Wichita anymore, sweetie," Mimi said. "And how are you going to stop me? Call nine-one-one?"

Chloe laughed.

"I-I'll tell one of the dockworkers!"

Mimi glared at her. "Okay. While you sacrifice yourself, we'll all run away and hide! Works for me! You think they'll understand what you're saying? Did you fail to notice no one minded that we were being walked, tied around the neck with rope? Does that seem civilized to you?"

"You want to sell us out when we just barely got away?" Chloe screeched.

"I said stealing is wrong, we're not going to do it." Hannah's pretty face screwed up in a mulish expression, cheeks red.

Acacia got right in her face. "Surviving is what we want to do. What do you think is going to happen to us? How many humans have you seen? Heard anyone speak English? Think someone will take us to the US Embassy? I don't think so!"

Mimi turned back to the container and pulled out some fabric. It was a huge jacket, in dark green. She put it on.

Hannah stamped her foot.

Chloe laughed, "What? Are you four?" She grabbed something out of the crate, too. Hannah slapped her face. Then everything happened at once. Chloe screamed as she fell down.

Mimi couldn't believe Hannah would hurt a kid like Chloe. She screamed, "You bitch!" and punched Hannah right in the mouth. Hannah went down like a rock.

Velvet started whistling, loud, high and anxious.

"You guys, stop it. Be quiet!" Acacia hissed.

"It's Velvet. Oh, I hope she's not hurt," Mimi pulled Velvet out of her shirt. Chloe started to cry harder. "She's okay, Chloe."

"You guys, someone heard! Get inside the crate and cover up." Acacia grabbed Chloe and shoved her into the crate. "Get in here!" she hissed at Mimi and Hannah. Mimi followed Acacia through the gap.

"Velvet looks okay to me, baby. I think she was just scared. Or maybe warning us." Mimi whispered to the sobbing Chloe.

"Get your ass in here, Hannah. You have no idea what they might do to you if they find you."

Mimi and Chloe looked at each other with wide eyes at Acacia's bad word.

Acacia reached out the hole, grabbed Hannah by the arm, and hauled her in. "And you are going to be quiet and not give us away. Getting us raped or killed is way worse than taking some clothes!

Chloe's only fourteen, for God's sake, and she's acting more mature than you!"

"Twelve, actually" Chloe confessed. "My birthday isn't until July. I was in seventh grade. I just pretended to be older to hang out with some kids."

"I figured," Mimi whispered and handed Velvet to Chloe for a cuddle. She gave Hannah a dirty look in the dim light of the container. "Only twelve and she's behaving better than you."

Hannah was sobbing and had a split lip. She sat down. Acacia covered her up and gave her a cloth for her bleeding lip.

"Everyone just be quiet for a while."

They all covered up with cloth and quieted down. Footsteps went by after a few minutes. They heard speaking, but not words they could understand.

They were quiet for a long time. Every time someone tried to talk, Acacia hushed them. They finally fell asleep to the distant noises of machinery in the soft piles of clothes.

***

"I wonder how long we slept?" Mimi asked. Acacia was awake, peering out the hole of the crate.

"I think we slept for a long time. Sleeping on those clothes was the best rest I've had since we got kidnapped. I woke up a while ago, there was a type of horn blast. Then a bunch of the alien workers walked down the path that way." She pointed. "I could hear their footsteps."

"Shift change, maybe?"

"Yes. Some other aliens came this way. Not as many as the number who left. There are fewer noises from the cranes and hauling machines. There must be a city down that path."

"I need to pee so bad."

"Um, I walked a couple aisles away and peed behind a big metal container. It was in shadow, so I figured no one would see me."

Mimi crawled out, looked around, and then found a shadowed area and did her business.

Acacia's pretty smart. We should elect her as leader or something. I'm too hot headed.

"How long have you been awake?"

"A couple hours," Acacia said. "I think, anyway. I'm one of those people who only sleep five hours or so. Drove my family mad when I was a kid until the doctor told them it was natural for me."

Everyone soon woke up. "Everyone whisper," Mimi said. "Sounds in the distance, probably workers on the path. We slept for hours, I think. You can sneak out to a shadowed spot and go pee. But be careful."

When everyone was back inside the crate, Mimi spoke. "I think we should choose Acacia as leader. She's smart, and she's not a hot head. Plus she's nice."

"Oh, I don't think I need to be leader!" Acacia protested.

"Yes, you do," said Chloe. "Mimi's right. I think we need to consider you our leader. Or whatever. Grand High Poobah. Queen of the Abducted."

Mimi took a deep breath. "I'm sorry I got so out of control. I shouldn't have hit you, Hannah."

Hannah wouldn't look at her.

"We need to whisper and be quiet. Look through the crate for things that might help us. I'm going to have a chat with Hannah." Acacia pulled Hannah to the shadows at the back of the crate. Mimi and Chloe could still hear them.

"Hannah, you're going to get us killed. Or somebody will steal us again," she said. "We need to hide and try to survive. I know you're in shock and still having a hard time believing this is happening. But you need to face it. This is reality now."

Hannah gave a sob. "I h-hate it so much."

Acacia gave her a hug. "I know. But I think it was Divine Providence that those worms got squashed, and we got away. Don't you? If we are sold as slaves to some alien, it would be so much worse! Now we need a plan so we can hide. Try and stay safe," Acacia said. "It's not like we can change anything that happened."

"No shit," whispered Chloe.

"I'm not going to do it," Hannah hissed. "I refuse to steal."

Anger welled up and Mimi climbed over the bins to the back. Chloe followed. "Then maybe you should head out of here on your own." Mimi's voice was a whisper, but hard.

Acacia gasped. Hannah's eyes got huge. Chloe whispered, "Go, girl."

Mimi rolled her eyes. "Look, Hannah. We have no resources, no friends, and no money. We don't know the language or even where we are. The rest of us all want to try to survive."

"Maybe we can find help," Hannah said with her head lowered.

"How? Where? Who do we trust? The guys that stuck needles in our eyes? The dockworkers who saw us walking on a leash?"

Hannah swallowed and wouldn't meet Mimi's eyes.

"Yeah, that's what I thought. You have no plan, and you want to pretend we're back in your comfy world. Well, look around." Mimi pointed out the crate opening to the gray ceiling that had a ship oozing through. "You're not the boss of anything here. We're just a bunch of-of dock rats! Poor homeless people. Trying to hide and survive. We need to take care of each other. And Chloe's only twelve. She's a child. We need to take care of her."

"I thought she was older," Hannah mumbled. "Sixteen."

"She wanted us to think that. But we three adults have a child to care for. Do you want a kid in the hands of slavers?"

Acacia hugged Hannah who started crying in big hard sobs.

"You tell Chloe you're sorry for hitting her, and we will all try harder to get along," Acacia said. "We are all different, lived different lifestyles, but for now we must stick together. Disguising ourselves with these clothes will help us be safe."

CHAPTER THREE

"I found a type of scissors, so we can get the rest of the rope off our necks." Chloe held up a large pair of sheers. It took a long time to saw through the rope still knotted around their necks.

"What a relief," Mimi said. The three of them went through the clothing while Hannah sat by herself near the opening. Mimi thought she might be crying and probably needed a moment to herself. They gave her the job of Look Out.

"I really want the four of us to stick together. I think being on our own would be even more dangerous. Strength in numbers, and all that," Acacia said.

"I agree. It is not going to be easy, but we need to be smart," Mimi said. "Who knows how close we got to tragedy."

"Within inches," Chloe said. "That splat could have been us."

They continued to go through the clothes. "Let's find things that aren't bright and showy," Acacia said. A few moments later, Hannah joined them, pulling out something brown and setting it aside.

"I wonder if these were costumes for a theater or something. All different styles and sizes, most of them colorful. Spangles, wigs," Mimi said.

Acacia found a case. Pots of color, powders, brushes.

"Makeup," Chloe said. She sounded reverent. "I can do my eyeliner."

Mimi scooted over to look at it. "I have an idea! We could make ourselves look different. You know, I was a theater minor. I've done a lot of makeup, did a kid's play with lots of animals. What if I did spots or something on our faces? So we look less human, less like the women who were tied together with the rope."

They agreed it was a good idea, so Mimi did makeup on all of them. Olive and tan around the hairline, dark brown around the eyes. Chloe wanted black eyeliner, but Mimi nixed that idea. "Some green, tan, and yellow splotches on the forehead and sides of cheeks. Brown on the lips, making them blend into our other skin."

"You, too, Hannah. I know you don't really want to be on your own," Acacia said.

Hannah nodded and let Mimi makeup her face.

They found dark cloaks with hoods, pull-on trousers, skirts and baggy shirts in the dullest colors they could find.

"I found a stapler thing," Mimi held it up. "What if we add parts of the wigs to the hoods. Fake hair."

The hoods were huge.

"We could use fabric to wrap around the hoods, so they fit tighter. Like a turban or headband?" Hannah said, rather subdued.

"Great idea," Acacia said.

Mimi smirked but cut strips of fabric. *Very shepherds at the Nativity scene,* she thought.

"I'm going to make bags using the stapler," Chloe said. "To hold the makeup and a change of clothes." The others helped by finding dark clothes. Soon they had bags with shoulder straps, big enough for lots of the clothing.

"So, now we are disguised. What next?" Mimi asked.

"I'm so hungry," Chloe said.

They were all silent for a while. "Don't even think of asking anyone for help. We need to blend in. Be unnoticed. Avoid looking at other people's faces," Mimi said.

"We go back to the ship. I think we received implants, maybe we will be able to understand the language soon," Acacia said

"How would we get back inside the ship?" Mimi asked. "They punched buttons on that panel on the side."

"I remember what they punched," Acacia said.

"You remember? How can you remember that?" Hannah asked.

"I don't know? I have a really good memory. Photographic, I think it's called."

"Well, let's go to the Wormship," Chloe said. "I need my kibble."

They walked cautiously out to the main path, waiting to get onto it when others were far away. They moved slowly back toward the Wormship, heads down, silent.

The area where the worms had been squished was clean, and looked like nothing had happened. The enormous ship that had distracted everyone on the dock was gone. Cranes were back at work. Aliens scurried around pushing floating carts and driving mover machines. No one paid any attention to them.

"Do you think the thing in our eyes did something? Like for reading?" Chloe asked.

"Maybe? Look at all these different races here. They have to be able to communicate, so they can do business," Acacia said.

"Can you read anything? There are signs everywhere," Mimi asked.

"No. Gives me a splitting headache to try," Acacia said after a moment.

They finally came to the ship. "It's bigger than I remember," Hannah said.

"I think it had more floors that we just didn't see," Acacia said. "Okay, let me try the pattern. Three on the top row. One on the second row. Two on the third row, one on the fourth row." The panel flickered with yellow light and the door swooshed open.

"Wormship, sweet Wormship," Chloe singsonged.

"Ugh, it stinks in here. If we could find more of that gel we could clean this room. That control area and bench are disgusting," Hannah said.

"You are so right. I'll help," Chloe said.

Acacia and Mimi stared at the girl, shocked. Chloe went right to the kibble container and started munching. "What?" she frowned at them. "I like clean places. My granny's house was nice. You should see some of the foster care dumps I've lived in. The group home I live in isn't too bad. The girls win treats for being tidy."

"You lived in a group home?" Mimi asked.

"Yeah, right around the corner from where we were kidnapped. For teen girls."

Everyone else helped themselves to kibbles, standing around the container since there was no clean place to sit.

"Okay, I have to ask," Hannah said. "What's Velvet?"

"Um. She's my pet. Or it. There's really no way to know if it's a boy or a girl," Mimi said. "I'll show her to you if you promise not to hurt her."

Hannah agreed, so Mimi brought out the small animal.

"I think she's a good watch dog," Chloe said. "She whistled when the container was swinging and when we were arguing and aliens started to walk by."

"Well, we need all the help we can get." Hannah said.

Mimi caught Acacia's eye. Hannah was going to work with them now.

After eating, they looked around. In the rear, out of sight from their cage, was a lift down to a lower level.

There were rooms. Storage rooms, mostly empty, though there were more barrels of their kibble and the gray powder the worms liked. A room that looked a bit like an office room, with consoles and chairs. A small crew room with six bunks built into the walls.

"Yay! They're not covered in worm poop," Chloe said.

***

Hannah threw down the cleaning cloth in the pile of other dirty cloths and sat down on the newly cleaned bench on the top deck. "Thank goodness that stench is gone! I think I had a continual migraine between the smell and that high-pitched whining sound."

"So you're feeling better now?" Acacia asked.
Hannah nodded.

"That's good. I think we've done all we can for this area as far as cleaning goes," Mimi said.

On the lower level they found some kind of tool like a wire cutter and had cut down the cage, rolled up the wire and put it down in a storage area.

The Wormship had an access to a lower utility area that was only about five foot to the ceiling. "We stay out of there!" Mimi said. "Too dangerous to explore. None of us know anything about engineering or mechanics. Dealing with alien engineering is probably a death sentence."

"I suggest we move downstairs into those crew quarters," Acacia said.

"Somehow I feel like somebody should be here on the console," Mimi said. "But what would we do? We don't know the languages, we don't know how to use the console. I just feel like, somehow, we should be keeping watch. Not that we could do anything."

"We could hit people over the head with those cutters," Chloe said, "If they have heads."

That made them smile. "Yeah, except I think they have laser guns," Acacia said. "I think you are in fight or flight mode, Mimi. We need to eat and get some real sleep. Maybe a real shower to help you relax. We have food, water, and shelter, at least for now."

They went down the narrow lift to the lower level. "I wonder how long this ship can stay in this space," Mimi said. "I'm sure there's some kind of fee."

"We should try to find out," said Hannah. "Maybe those implants will start working, and we'll understand some of the speech around us."

"There's a screen of some type downstairs in the office room. I thought I'd play with it because I don't think it would do anything to the engines," Mimi said.

"Maybe we can find a news channel or something," Acacia said. "If we hear the language more, perhaps we'll begin to understand it."

"That's a good point," said Mimi. "Let's try that."

They went down the narrow lift to the crew quarters on the lower level. One large room had bunks built into the wall, about seven feet long by three feet, with a padded mattress.

"I don't think the worms built this ship," Acacia said. "They wouldn't need beds this long."

"I'm going to make a pillow," said Chloe. "I'm glad we brought all the fabric, even the bright stuff. I'm going to make my pillow lime green." She dug out the fabric stapler found with the clothing and proceeded to make a rectangle. She stuffed it with bright turquoise cloth. "Want me to make you guys one? Seriously, this is the most fun I've had in months."

"Sure, make me one. I don't care what color," Mimi said.

Chloe was soon busy with the stapler and clothes. Mimi watched her, realizing that she wasn't really one of the women, she was a kid. And they were responsible for her. She glanced at Acacia. They both shared the recliner in front of the screen while Hannah went to the showers.

"Chloe seems so young," Mimi whispered.

"Weren't we all at twelve?"

"I wonder what kind of careers there are, out here. Back home she'd be busy with school."

"Holy cow, Mimi, I think we could hold off on that for a few months, until we kind of have an idea how to survive here." Acacia gave her an exasperated look. "Let's not pile on the trouble right now. Let's keep things simple."

Mimi took a deep breath, "You're right. Yes, let's not bite off more than we can chew."

Hannah came back from the showers. "I found the bolt of cloth that the worms gave us." It was plain, heavy tan fabric. "I'll make more, you know, pads for our upcoming red flood tomorrow," Hannah said.

Chloe said. "I'll help tomorrow. They'll be nicer than our old ones. I think I'll get ready for bed right now, though. You think it's bedtime? I sure miss toothpaste."

"I think there's enough here that we can all have a blanket, too," Hannah said. "I'll cut one for you while you shower." She proceeded to cut them each a blanket about six feet long, and a pile of rectangles to make into pads.

"She's trying," Acacia mouthed into Mimi's ear. Mimi nodded.

Chloe hopped onto a top bunk and Hannah tossed her a blanket. "Oh, wow. I feel like a real human again," Chloe murmured.

Mimi and Acacia had no luck with the screen, though Acacia did find the light dimmer. They showered in a real shower and went to bed.

Mimi woke feeling better than she had since their abduction. She ate a cupful of kibble and washed it down with hot water since there was no cold water on the ship. She and Acacia went back to the screen. After Hannah got up, Hannah and Chloe went upstairs to wash the walls. "I'm sure the worms left filth all over the top floor," Hannah said.

"Yeah, gives me the heebie jeebies!" Chloe bounded to the lift.

Later, Hannah offered to wash all their ordinary clothes, so they donned the strange baggy clothes from the crate. Chloe cut long strips of bright fabric, poked holes in their tan blankets and decorated them with weavings and bows.

"That's pretty," Acacia said. "I never would have thought of that."

"There's really nothing else to do," Chloe said.

Acacia gasped. "Lordy Pete, why didn't I think of this earlier?" She went to the wall panel and started punching buttons. The screen on the small console came on. After some fiddling they found a button that took them to different channels.

Finally, they came to a channel with someone speaking against the backdrop of an odd city. The speaker was one of the elephant nose kind of guys, the ones with the big eyes and the long lashes.

"I want to figure out how to turn up the volume," Acacia said. They proceeded to touch all the buttons and knobs until finally the volume came on.

"Okay let's see if this makes any sense," Mimi said.

"It seems like he's talking about those buildings," Hannah said.

"We haven't seen any buildings like that," Chloe said.

"We've only seen the space dock. There's probably a whole city," Acacia said. "A planet."

Mimi sighed. "I still can't understand a word. Maybe those ear shots weren't translators at all."

Acacia nodded. "Maybe the more we hear it, the more sense it will make? Keep it on in the background? Background sounds actually make things seem more normal for me," Acacia said. "My grandparents had the TV on every waking hour. It was never quiet."

"Not really quiet here," Hannah said. "We can hear clanging and banging from the cranes and the crates."

"Yeah. What I really don't want to hear is somebody knocking on our door asking for rent money," Acacia said.

That idea hung over their heads, even Chloe's. In their search through the Wormship they had found a small drawer with about 20 cubes in it. Hannah called them cubits, which made sense to everybody. "So we have twenty cubits. We have no idea what they are worth," Mimi said.

"The worms paid six for each of us at the implant place," Acacia said. "I counted."

"Really? I was in so much pain I couldn't even think," Hannah said.

"I concentrated since I thought it might be important."

"That was probably a lot of money for electronics, so food might be less. I wonder if we have enough here to pay more rent on the ship."

"I wish there was a way we could earn money. Things are always better if you have lots of money," Mimi said. "Not that I've ever had lots of money, just saying."

"You're right. If we could earn some money, we'd be in a better position no matter what happened," Acacia said.

"I'll make little belts with the pockets. We should carry the cubits with us, in case they take the ship or something," Chloe said.

"Good idea." Mimi said.

"Let's split the money up, too. Just to be safe." Acacia said.

"Chloe, show me how you want to make them, and I'll help," Hannah said.

Acacia and Mimi searched the screen while Hannah and Chloe made the pocket belts. Chloe hummed a song while she stapled the fabric.

"I've got it!" Mimi said. "A way for us to make money."

They all looked at her.

"This is going to sound kind of strange, but a month before the kidnapping I went to visit some friends in Chicago. They moved up there to get jobs in theater, and they do get acting jobs now and then. In between working at coffee shops and waitressing, one of the things a couple of them do is busk. You know, they take their guitars and sing in the streets and people put money in their guitar case. They go to a busy area downtown, like when there are lots of people around and people toss dollar bills. It's not a lot of money, but they save it up for the rent or go out to eat."

"Well, we don't have any guitars," Hannah said.

"No, but didn't you two sing in the choir? Chloe can sing, and I'm okay, have been in a couple musicals. So what if we sang a song? If we can find a busy place away from the docks."

"There must be a marketplace in that city the reporters talk about," Acacia said. "What if we went there and put something out with like one cubit in it? To give people the idea of what they should do."

"I always thought it was kind of like begging," Hannah said.

"No, it's not." Mimi disagreed. "The arts are worthy of pay. Music is not always free like choir."

"That's true," Acacia said.

"Okay, then I'll consider it."

"But what would we even sing?" Acacia asked.

"Acacia and I know church songs. You two won't know them."

"We all know Christmas songs," Mimi said. "We can sing "Silent Night" and other songs everybody knows. "America the Beautiful". It won't matter to all the aliens."

Acacia turned around in her recliner and looked at them. "You know that's not a bad idea, because Hannah and I know the parts for different Christmas songs. Hannah knows a pretty descant for "Silent Night." I know the alto part."

They practiced for quite a while, and got three songs together, plus a peppy version of "Rudolph."

"Let's sleep and then look for a busy place," Acacia said.

***

"What if it's illegal?" Hannah asked.

"Well," Mimi said. "Walking women around tied by the neck with a rope was not illegal, so I suspect the laws are pretty lax. I'm not talking about doing it around the docks, where we might be underfoot. We need to walk farther down the path and get to like a market area or place with restaurants."

"Does everyone know the pattern to unlock the ship's door?" Acacia asked. "Just in case we get separated, work your way back here! Don't wander around, just stick to main roads." They all practiced unlocking the door, which was a good thing because Mimi and Hannah had no clue.

"As a back-up meeting spot, find the broken crate," Mimi said.

"Come on, let's find a place to make us some money," Chloe said.

"If this was a scifi book, there would be a ship's tutorial on how to fly, and one of us would be a natural," Acacia said with a sigh.

"Not our luck. At least we have kibble and cool makeup," Chloe said. "And a cute alien pet."

"You're certainly chipper," Mimi said.

"Well, yeah. We killed it with the harmony last night."

Mimi didn't have a great voice, but she had been in several musicals in high school and college and was capable of learning a part. She sang alto with Acacia, who had a rich, lovely voice. Chloe sang second soprano or the melody with Hannah. Hannah had a pretty, high soprano voice. They dressed and made-up carefully for the performance and headed past the dock area.

"Don't make eye contact with anybody," Hannah said. "We don't want them to think we're trying to-to solicit or something." So they were silent, heads bowed. No one seemed to notice them at all.

Finally, the women came to a station-type place. The doors swooshed open in front of people ahead of them, and they followed them into a brightly lit, high ceiling space.

Several paths stretched ahead of them, each one encased in its own clear tube. The paths stopped for people to walk on, and then a gate came up and the path full of people zipped away.

"Which one do we take, Mimi?" Acacia asked.

"Let's take the one that has the most people on it. They must be going somewhere."

To their surprise the moving path didn't cost them anything. They just walked up onto it, and then they sat down on a bench and watched everything go by though the clear tube walls. They were all shocked when the path went over areas of open space. They could even see spaceships flying underneath. The dock behind them was actually a huge spiral with different levels of spiral arms. Ahead of them they saw a planet, green, lavender, and white.

"Wow this place is huge! There must be millions of people there," Mimi said. "This path doesn't seem to be going that fast."

"Maybe it's going faster than we think," Acacia said.

There were no seat belts or harnesses and all the surrounding people acted as if this was just an everyday thing. Crossing through space from a space station to a planet, ordinary.

"Look," said Chloe. "There's a moon."

It seemed much closer than the moon from Earth, larger.

"That kind of freaks me out," Chloe said.

"I wonder if it has green grass like Earth?" Hannah asked.

"I guess we'll find out." As they got closer, the clouds spread out a little and they could see a glimpse of the land below them. There was green, and the blue of water. They also saw purple and gold.

"It doesn't look like Earth," said Chloe.

As the tube got even closer, they realized that the large swaths of purple were some type of forest. They came near a city. Individual buildings began to stand out as they moved down to street level, buildings sweeping by. "I guess we were going fast," Mimi said.

Then the tube ride slowed to a halt in an area similar to the one they had entered to get on.

"Let's just follow the crowd out and see what we can find," Mimi said.

"Whatever you do, try to remember how to get back to this station. We were on the center tube path," Acacia cautioned. "Because it's not like we can ask anyone for directions."

The four followed the aliens, and then to their left they saw a large plaza area with greenery, purple leaf trees, outdoor eateries with chairs and tables and a park area with shrubs.

"Jackpot!" Mimi said.

"It isn't grass," Chloe said. "Kind of like round clover." The shrubs had dark bark but were kind of like a willow in the way they drifted down. The leaves were purple with white underneath. "That's really pretty," said Chloe. "Let's call that Purple Park."

"All right so from the Purple Park we go straight toward that white rectangle building, and then we turn right to get back to the center tube path," Acacia said.

People of all species sat at tables eating and drinking while others went into shops. Purple Park had seating areas and tables. "I think those are little kids playing in a play area," Hannah said

"That's definitely a playground. Look, it has soft stuff underneath so if kids fall, they won't get hurt," Chloe said. Swings and climbers were not all that different from a park on Earth.

"I think we should go over to the side of the park that's close to all those tables full of people eating and sing," Mimi said. "No time like the present."

"I'm so nervous," said Chloe.

"You'll do great," Mimi reassured her.

"Hey, look at those aliens at that long table. They look almost human."

"Devil horns," Hannah gasped.

Chloe turned to her with scorn. "They're brown, not red! Sheesh. Two eyes, a mouth, human-type nose and hair."

"Oh my, did you see that alien's eyes light up?" Mimi discretely pointed out a different table with human-like aliens. Some had three eyes, though.

Acacia said, "They could have mechanical parts. Computers. Like cyborgs."

"Let's just sing," Hannah said. "Get it over with."

They sang "Silent Night", followed by "God Rest Ye Merry Gentlemen," and "Go Tell It on the

Mountain." Aliens noticed them immediately. Chloe held up the bag she had made especially for collecting money and tossed two cubits in it. After several songs, a trunk-faced couple walked up and tossed in some cubes.

"It worked. I can't believe it worked," Chloe said.

"Let's move over there and sing again," Mimi said. She was quite pleased at the number of cubits tossed into the bag. They crossed the park to sing closer to the restaurants. Mimi scooped out the money and tucked it away in the pocket, so it always looked like they only had a couple cubits.

CHAPTER FOUR

They sang in one area and made several cubits, then moved closer to the outdoor dining. Two children left their table and came to listen.

The children looked nearly human, with dark curly hair and tan skin. The small girl wore a red sheer scarf over her forehead, which obscured a third eye, closed, in the middle of her forehead. All had three long fingers and a human type thumb, though none had fingernails.

They were accompanied by enormous cat-like animals. Their fur was almost non-existent, just on the ears and tail, and they had snakelike skin. Two were black and one had the same markings as an orange tabby, only in snakeskin, not fur.

As the children listened to their selection of carols, their already striking hazel eyes lit up like light bulbs. Hannah, who stood right behind Mimi, clutched her arm. Mimi could tell by the way she lost all breath control that Hannah was upset or scared.

Suddenly Chloe yelled, "Velvet!" Velvet had leaped out of Mimi's normal place in a pocket in her belt. She scampered across the white walkway and leaped on one of the lizard cats, chirping and whistling the whole time.

The children tossed a handful of cubits in the cloth hat and went back to their table, with Velvet riding on one of the lizard-cat things.

"Velvet! Hey, that's my pet!" Mimi took off at a run, followed by Chloe. Acacia had the presence of mind to snatch up the money before they all ran. Mimi careened to a halt in front of a long table of adults who resembled the children. Various light bulb glowing eyes turned to them. The children spoke excitedly, and Mimi braved the cat thing and snatched Velvet off its head.

"I hear that you sing Earth songs in English." A man spoke in English with a thick accent. He had brown skin, dark curls and human features, except for the glowing blue eyes. His hands were five fingered human hands, though several at the table only had three long fingers and a thumb. A woman, wearing a sheer blue scarf covering a closed third eye smiled at them. Her skin had a teal tint, her teeth were blinding white.

"Um. Yes. You speak English," Mimi said through her shock.

The man nodded. "Yes. We are the Valryssian family." He frowned at them. "You don't look particularly like an Earthling. My brother Tris looks more Terran than you." He waved at a young man who smiled. His glowing eyes changed to normal hazel green, and he looked completely human, even his hands.

"We're wearing makeup. And this white hair...it is just part of our costume," Chloe explained, pulling on the hair.

"I see."

He waved at a server. "Why don't we go inside to a large private table? We can talk. I, of course, will pay for the meal."

Acacia looked at the others, who nodded. "Oh, yes, thank you."

Several servers carried away the food and they entered a large restaurant. The servers led them to the side, to a room with windows overlooking the Purple Park.

The Valryssian man spoke to the servers and soon they brought more food. "Help yourselves. We can tell you what the dish is called."

They served themselves a bit of everything.

"I am Kyre Valryssian, First Officer of the ship Red Haven," he said. "My brothers, Tris and Trineal Valryssian. Trineal's lovely bride Zhuzhana, and my older brother's children, Galileo, Cassien and Theless Valryssian. We are traders, visiting Fera for business."

"I'm Acacia, this is Hannah, Mimi and Chloe. This planet is called Fera?" Acacia said while everyone served food.

"How did you get here from Earth?" Kyre asked.

"Aliens kidnapped us. How do you know about Earth?" Mimi asked.

"Not many do. It is not part of the Trade Alliance." He took a sip of his drink. "My family has an Earth ancestor. He taught us English and Deutsch, which we use within the family. No others know it, so we have privacy."

"Earth sent people to space years ago?" Acacia asked, eyes wide.

Kyre grinned. "Not really. Our ancestor sent himself to space in a homemade rocket and with homemade fuel. He was a man ahead of his time. I can tell you the whole story sometime, but right now I want to know how you got to Fera."

"Well, they were wormy things, with lots of tiny hairy feet. Or hands. Greenish and really stinky. They leaked brown stuff," Mimi said,

"I'm sure it was kaka," Chloe said.

"We all happened to be on the same street one evening, back on Earth. A worm hit us with pink ray, and we woke in a cage on their ship."

"Shikshiks," Tris said. "Whooee. The stench."

"We cleaned a lot to get rid of the smell and stains," Hannah said.

"Shikshiks have a reputation for theft and other illegal activities," Kyre said. "Piracy."

"So slavery isn't illegal here? The worms had us tied around the neck with ropes when they took us to get the ear and eye shots," Mimi said.

Kyre was silent for a moment. "You were on Grzbt? The large space dock?"

"I guess so? It was a dock with lots of ships. We took a tube transportation to get here."

"Grzbt is a commercial space station. It is a lawless place, though Fera wants to regulate it. Slavery is illegal on Fera. It has a system of law and the military to back it up. We have our ship within Fera's legal space. Grzbt is right outside the boundary."

"Sounds like you got translator and reader chips," Tris said.

"They don't work," Acacia said. "We don't understand anything."

"I could check them," he offered.

"He's a tech," Kyre said. "So how did you get away from the Shikshiks?"

"By accident," Mimi said. She wasn't sure what was wrong with her. It was like she couldn't catch her breath. She was...stunned. English speakers.

And he was good-looking, too.

"No shit," Chloe added. Acacia raised her eyebrows at Chloe, who ducked her head.

Acacia rolled her eyes and took over. "We were walking along the path where ships are parked after getting the ear and eye shots. Tied together with the ropes around our necks. A crane accidentally dropped a container right on top of the worms, freeing the rope. We ran and hid in the containers, a long way from the accident. We slept for a night in a broken crate. Then we found our disguises and went back to the Wormship. We had no other means to get food and shelter."

Kyre looked at them with raised eyebrows and his eyes turned from human hazel green to bright blue lights. "I think I should accompany you back to your ship, but I need to contact Rhodes, my oldest brother. He is the captain of our ship."

His eye lights flickered to green. "Rhodes, you'll never believe this. We met four Earth women, stranded on Grzbt. Yes, completely human, abducted from Earth. They speak English, and their translators don't work. Shikshiks abducted them, but they died when a container fell on them. They have some small spacecraft. I want to check it." He paused and listened, eyes flashing. "A couple more would be good."

His eyes changed back to human hazel. "Rhodes is sending cousins down for additional guards. I know my brothers, Zhuzhana, and the children wish to shop, but I think it is important to check your ship, to see how secure you are."

"We are worried we will need to pay rent. We have some cubes, but don't know the money here or when payment is due," Mimi told him.

They finished the meal with a sweet cake with cream and cups of a hot drink, not quite tea or coffee, but not bad. Mimi gave Velvet some cake.

"I see you have a nanosnoot," Kyre said.

"Oh, that's what they are called?"

"Yes. They are creations of my clan but have spread to many ships and space docks. The parent nanos are transmitted to the kits. They clean invasive nano particles from equipment and computers. Most ships have many, because a competitor might send malicious nanobotss. Pirates also use nanotech to disable ships."

Three more Valryssians arrived, and the shoppers left.

Two of the newcomers looked like the family, so they must be related. The third had the same skin tone, wavy dark hair, and hazel eyes but also had an elephant trunk nose. His eyes had the very long, heavy eyelashes they had noticed the trunk people had.

"All right, reinforcements are here. These are my cousins Alyxin, Zaver, and Strongbow. We want to see how much rental time your ship has and what shape it is in. We might be able to move it to a more secure place."

The meal finished, and they followed Kyre and the other men to the path that would lead to the spacedock. The men were accompanied by more of those long-legged cat-creatures. One of the creatures had plush gray stripes and looked a lot more like an Earth house cat, only on longer legs.

"Can I ask what those things are?" Mimi asked.

"Oh, those are hybrids with Earth cats. When my great-grandfather, Wilhelm Heinz, left Earth, he lived in the country and had some sheds with wild house cats. He left in a rocket and didn't realize that a kitten had climbed in with him until he had already launched.

"Eventually, he lived on a planet called Doona. His cat was a female and became very tame. He named her Gloria. She had kittens that were part Night Hunter, a denizen of planet Doona. A kind of long-legged, leather-skinned predator with triangular ears. They hunt in packs. The kittens were an odd mix, but they became loyal pets. They can be quite formidable if someone attacks. That's why we always have them with the family when we're on a planet. When we're home on the ship, they beg for food and do whatever they like."

"Like a regular cat."

He grinned. "Probably, but I have never met a full Earth cat. Your nanosnoot is safe with them, by the way. They consider snoots to be part of their pack. Compatible technology."

"You live in space on a ship?"

"Yes, mostly. We are traders and live in large ships, like cities."

"So humans can have children with aliens?" Mimi asked.

"They can with some aliens, the humanoid ones. My ancestor was saved from certain death by the Valryssian Clan, who are Trengulu people. Trengulu females have the third eye. There are several races of humanoids. Our clan has members with ancestry of many. Strongbow is part Kulag." He indicated the trunk nosed man.

"Wait, do you have people that are small with big ears?" Chloe asked.

"A few on my homeship. Their race is called Aliarietts."

"There are also space lanes that don't draw a lot of humanoids. You have your bird-type people, Bisk's," he said.

"What about the things that brought us here, the worms?"

"Oh, the worms. They are from a world that is not a part of the Trade Alliance. Basically have no ethics. Or they believe every being not a Shikshik is prey. Impossible to do business with."

He drew a deep breath. "I am a little concerned that they found Earth. I wonder if it was purposeful or if it was an accident."

"Yes, I wonder if we should set a few drones up in that system. I could see the Shikshik causing a lot of trouble for Earthlings since they do not yet have spaceflight," Alyxin said

"Well, we got to the Moon in 1969," Chloe said.

"Really? We might send someone to investigate Earth's space abilities. It might be best if they were introduced to the space lanes by someone like us, not by someone like the worms," he replied.

"Yeah, if the Earth doesn't blow itself up first," Chloe said. "The leaders of the world don't seem to be showing a lot of concern."

"We know that there are troubled, warlike planets and systems poorly run. We try to work with the well-run ones," Kyre said. "Better for trade."

As they spoke, they got into the tube and shot toward the space dock. They finally got to the ship. It looked shabbier than ever, surrounded by much newer, well cared for ships.

"Shikshik, all right. Their ships are often in poor condition," Alyxin said.

"This is really an antique," Strongbow said in a deep voice. "I think this is a Stansan Trader, probably two or three hundred years old. You were lucky to even get here in one piece. The Stansan are a humanoid race that rarely use space flight."

Acacia punched the security buttons, and they entered the ship.

"You have done a good job of cleaning it. I don't smell the worm stench at all," Kyre said.

"Thanks, it was a lot of work, but that stink was confined to this level. They never went to the level below with actual bunks and bathrooms."

"We lived in a cage. We took it down," said Mimi indicating the area where the cage had been.

Kyre stared at the area for a moment, then went to the console. "Let's see how much time you have left on your rent."

He turned on the console. It wasn't long before he had data on a screen.

"The Shikshiks paid thirty thousand steles for this space and your term of service is up in two standard days."

"That's not good," Mimi said.

"I'm calling my brother Rhodes, since we are on a short timeline."

He and his brother talked back and forth about mechanics, docks.

"Rhodes is sending a tug. They can bring the ship safely to Red Haven, where we have docking space in our repair bays. Our mechanics can work on it. Rhodes invites you to join us on Red Haven, in our housing area. It is pleasant there in our apartment complex. You all will be more comfortable and safe. We won't be in a rush to get you situated somewhere in Fera space."

"So what would we do on your ship?" Acacia asked.

Kyre looked at them. "Eventually, you could find jobs on board. Everybody eventually works or trains for a position. But let's be realistic. You're not trained for living in space. Before anything else, you need your translator chips to work. After that, we can teach you our technology or skills specific to a career interest. Classes and tutorials would keep you occupied for some time."

"You don't think you could get us back to Earth?" Hannah asked.

"I don't think so. We are part of the Allied Systems Trade Treaty. Our code of conduct forbids us from interaction with worlds that are not yet in space."

"Star Trekky," Acacia whispered.

"I know we have a probe sent to Mars, would that count?" Hannah looked a bit teary eyed.

"No, I'm sorry," Kyre said. "You'd actually have to live outside your solar system. Not probes or satellites."

He was quite gentle with Hannah, who did look heartbroken.

Mimi was conflicted. She was glad he seemed to be a kind man, but Mimi suddenly noticed Hannah was actually quite pretty once you ignored her personality. Kyre might like her. Many men might.

Mimi gave herself a mental slap. *This is no time in life to be thinking about a man you just met! An alien man!*

"It's not completely hopeless, and you might find life quite fulfilling with the Valryssian Clan. We're law-abiding types, everybody has food and clothing, medical care, education. Safety."

Acacia reached out for Hannah. "I think we need to talk, ladies." She looked at Kyre. "We want to run downstairs and discuss this in private."

"Certainly."

The four of them went down to the crew quarters on the lower level.

"We have to do it." Acacia said. "We can't stay here. I don't know how much steles are worth, but I'm pretty sure we haven't earned thirty thousand by singing in the park."

"They do seem civilized, I guess," said Hannah, whose eyes were red. "I'll be honest. This dock area frightens me. The way people look at us as we walked by. I'm afraid that we might just end up with a different group of slavers."

Mimi looked at her in surprise, since it was the most Hannah had spoken in months.

"I actually agree with Hannah," said Chloe. "We are no way safe here. It is yucky to have to be rescued by other people, but this will be much nicer than the group home I lived in. Some of those girls were pure mean."

"I don't think we have the skills to pull off long-term survival here on our own," Acacia said. "Our education is too primitive."

"I think you're right. So we go with them?" Mimi asked.

The four agreed to go to Red Haven.

They told Kyre of their decision. "We don't want to be a burden on you, and hopefully we'll be able to pay back your kindness," Acacia said.

Kyre smiled. Nice smile, Mimi noted. "I am certain you will be wonderful members of Red Haven."

He checked a hologram that popped up from a wristband. "It would be safer if you return to Red Haven with us on our transport. The tugs are not as safe as our transport ship. We have living quarters that I'm sure you would find sufficient."

"Trust me, we are not that attached to the Wormship." Mimi grinned at him and was delighted when he grinned back.

After that, everything went in a blur. Chloe insisted they bring the bags with the pillows and blankets, so they packed the few things they had. Mimi packed kibble for Velvet.

They walked back to the tube paths and returned to Fera. Kyre communicated with his brothers and sister-in-law about the state of their shopping, and they decided they would all meet in an hour at the transport ship area.

"The ship we're using is a standard passenger transport. Not large, but it is quite comfortable. We can relax and have refreshments while waiting for the others."

They rode to the Fera spaceport on another moving sidewalk, similar to the tube-paths. Instead of running underground like a subway, it was on scaffolding high above the city, which made for a scenic ride.

"Fera is beautiful," Mimi said.

"It is a resort planet, quite expensive in the cities. When I was a boy, I attended children's camp out in the countryside. Lovely there," Kyre said.

They parked in front of a white ship, triangular in shape. "Come on in. You can relax with drinks. There are hygiene facilities towards the back."

CHAPTER FIVE

This ship was nothing like the Wormship. Its interior was white, the chairs upholstered in dark red plush. Kyre brought out flavored waters and small cookies.

They used a clean, well stocked restroom. Chloe was thrilled with the sweet-smelling cleanser and scrubbed her face clean of the animal makeup. "It smells so good."

Mimi gave Velvet a moment in the cool water while she scrubbed off her own makeup. Chloe returned with her. "The bathroom has actual soap to wash your hands and face." Chloe waved her hands in front of Hannah. Hannah grinned.

Mimi goggled at her a moment, *Hannah can grin?* Then she grinned, too. "Doesn't even leave your face feeling tight."

Hannah is changing, warming up. I need to be nicer. She's not some kind of monster. Maybe she's not so flexible, but that doesn't make her a bad person.

Soon the shoppers returned and got ready for the flight. All their purchases were put down below through a small hatch.

Kyre and his brothers went into a room at the front of the ship, but Kyre soon returned to the passenger seats.

There was a bell followed by a voice speaking an unknown language.

"Please harness, in case of gravity fluctuations," Kyre translated.

They harnessed and Mimi leaned her chair back like a recliner. She closed her eyes for just a moment, feeling a sense of relief that they would be all right. She had spent many nights awake, worrying. Acacia had, also. Mimi peeked at her in the seat across the aisle with Hannah, and saw she was yawning in her seat.

"I'm taking a snooze. Unless this is scary," Chloe said, sitting next to her.

Kyre grinned. "Not scary, very routine. I often nap." He checked to see everyone was harnessed, then went back to the flight control room.

The take-off seemed just like an airplane to Mimi. Chloe shut her eyes and slept like the child she was, leaning against the ship's wall. Kyre entered the passenger area from the flight room where his two brothers remained. "Stay harnessed, please. We will experience a bit of turbulence in a few minutes. Normal. Nothing to be alarmed about," he told everyone. He sat down in the seat next to Mimi and harnessed himself.

An unexpected warmth spread through her. She mentally groaned. *A crush, really? With a four fingered part-alien with Christmas-light eyes?*

His arm brushed hers, and every follicle on her body stood at attention.

This is what I get for swearing off men until I graduate. The first attractive guy to come along...

"I will speak with my brother Rhodes when we get to Red Haven. Alyxin and I think the Trade Alliance Council needs to know the Shikshik have found Earth, and have enslaved people."

"Can they stop them?"

"Not sure. But the Shikshik are not known for exploration or navigation skills. They may have followed another ship. The Alliance Guard can set up a boundary."

He was quiet then, checking things on the holoscreen computer on his wrist. Mimi drifted to sleep.

A jerk and a shout woke her abruptly. "What is happening?"

"I don't know." Chloe's eyes were huge. The Valryssians slumped, unconscious in their seats. "They are all asleep."

"Unconscious," Mimi said after trying to wake Kyre. None of the four Earth women felt any different.

"There's a tube stuck to the wall, by the chair leg. See it?" Acacia pointed out a small needle-nosed tube. "I heard a hiss, like a car tire with a leak. Knockout gas?"

The ship moved erratically for some time.

"Hide," Mimi said. "I think we are being abducted."

"Again?" Hannah groaned.

"There must be cupboards or storage."

There was quite a bit of noise, clanking of machinery, whining sounds. Hydraulics, maybe.

"There's a hatch in the floor." Acacia's voice was tense. " Where they put their purchases." Acacia found the hatch and opened it. "It goes to the storage area with small stairs."

"Chloe, you first. Hannah,go," Mimi gently moved them toward the hatch.

Chloe went down the stairs, Hannah followed. "Luggage area," Hannah called up.

The murder cats were still awake. Mimi got their attention and pointed at the opening. "You should hide."

One of the murder cats, the fluffy one, grabbed the sleeve of one of the sleeping children and tugged. It glared at Mimi.

"Yeah, okay." She grabbed the child, who didn't weigh much. "Catch this kid," She called down and lowered the child down to Hannah while Acacia grabbed another. "Try to hide them. I want to try and get Kyre. Since none of us know anything. Maybe we can wake him up."

They got the three small children down, and the murder cats leaped down the hole gracefully.

Acacia and Mimi got Kyre onto the aisle floor and dragged him by his feet to the access hole.

"What is this guy made of? Lead?" Acacia moaned.

"He's really heavy. If the three of you try to hold him, I'll try to lower him," Mimi said.

"Honestly, Mimi. I think I'm stronger, you're just a little minnow. Get down the ladder, and I'll lower him."

Mimi acknowledged that Acacia was eight inches taller than her, and likely outweighed her by fifty pounds.

Acacia used a sash from her clothing under his arms, which helped a lot. Still, it was hard work shifting his dead weight around. Acacia finally came down the ladder, and Mimi closed the hatch.

"Hide behind stuff." She and Acacia pulled the unconscious children behind a metal crate fastened to the grating that covered the floor and walls.

Chloe had dragged the cloth bags with her. Mimi piled and draped their blankets and clothes over everyone, rearranging baggage to hide them better. Then she squeezed in a narrow space behind a tall rectangular crate next to Acacia.

"Port hole," Acacia, whispered and pulled up a folding metal shade.

They were in space, but a robotic arm had hold of the transport and dragged it toward an open doorway on a space ship. "That's the ship we saw right before the accident, the one everyone stared at," Acacia whispered. "The huge one."

It was. Enormous, oblong, gleaming silver with gold trim. At one end were huge circular forms.

The transport was pulled closer and closer to the ship. The doorway opened into a large hold into which the robotic arms moved them. The transport landed with a thump in the hold. Mimi heard the whoosh and clunk of the door shutting. The transport was moved into place with clanks and jerks. "Probably locking the ship down," Acacia whispered.

Then nothing.

"Maybe they need to pressurize the hold. You know, air." Acacia said.

A murder cat poked its head into their hiding place. Mimi glanced at Acacia. "Hi."

The cat stretched out a lethal looking paw and pricked her arm with one claw. "Ow!"

Velvet leaped out of her belt and touched the cat's paw and Mimi's hand.

Then she saw something. Odd perspective. Everything was colorless, except a small door or hatch surrounded by blue light. It was in the floor.

"Is that a way out?" Mimi asked

"Ysss," the cat whispered in her head.

"Acacia, the cat mind speaks. Telepathy. He is showing me a small door in the floor."

"Shhheee."

"Sorry. It's a female."

"The wall is lifting." Acacia said. "We're next to a storage room. Huge. Enormous. We'll hide for now, and then we'll try to get out."

Velvet gave warning chirps.

"Hide, everyone," Mimi whispered.

Acacia kept watch through the small porthole. "They are humanoid. Six fingers, copper metallic skin and hair. Armor. Bony foreheads and noses. I guess they are noses."

"I've seen some copper people," Chloe whispered.

The transport door to the passenger area opened, then thuds of footsteps pounded above them.

There was another swoop. Mimi could see a door on one end open. She scrunched as low as she could behind the crate, pulling her cloak over her face. *Don't wake up now*, she silently commanded the sleeping Valryssians, who were barely breathing, so movement wouldn't show. The door swooped closed.

"He didn't see us." Hannah sounded shocked.

The lizard cats crawled over them, thankfully with claws retracted, to the hatch. They all snapped their tails expectantly.

"Like cats, but so much scarier," Mimi whispered.

"Chloe, Hannah, we're going through another hatch. There is a crate area, try to get to it and hide. You two go through first and Acacia and I will get the little kids and Kyre."

The hatch was much harder to open, and was more like a tube. When the door opened there was a handle, and Mimi pulled up a four-foot section of fluffy stuff caged in wire. "Insulation," Acacia whispered. Instead of stairs there was a narrow ladder.

Hannah and Chloe climbed down. Mimi and Acacia handed the sleeping children down.

"We are under the ship," Hannah whispered up to them.

Again, they wrestled Kyre down the tube to the floor below. He dropped, but Chloe and Hannah kept his head from banging on the metal grid of the floor.

The murder cats came down on their own and streaked for the storage area. "Okay, Hannah, Chloe, and I will get the kids across." Mimi told Acacia. "You stay with Kyre, and I'll come back to help drag him. Quick, before someone comes back."

Acacia grabbed the bags and blankets. She handed Hannah the cloth. "Put the blankets under the kids and pull."

Chloe grabbed a small child, positioned her on a blanket, and scuttled backward toward the storage area, pulling her across. Hannah and Mimi followed with the other small children.

"I'm going back to help Acacia," Mimi whispered.

"I'll come, too. He's super heavy," Hannah said.

Acacia had rolled Kyre onto a large black cloak. Pulling him across the ceramic floor was much easier than moving him down the stairs or the hatch.

"Let's move back into the middle of these containers," Acacia whispered. They found a space surrounded on three sides by large packing crates.

Velvet, in Mimi's pocket, suddenly leaped onto her chest and whistled softly.

"Everyone, quiet. God, I wish I could see something."

A murder cat, the fluffier one, stood guard with them. One of the cats leaped on top of the crate close to the walkway. Another cat gently touched Velvet. No claw for Velvet, Mimi noticed.

Mimi could *see*. Two float trucks, similar to haulers used on the docks, came through the storage area to the Valryssian's transport ship. Two men in armored suits and helmets opened the ship and unloaded all the goods from the transport to the float. The men on the second float piled the Valryssians, still asleep, onto their hauler and took off, followed by the other hauler. With a swoosh a wall slammed down, blocking the transport ship from the storage area. Small clamps on the floor latched onto the wall.

She breathed. "They took Kyre's family and the contents of the ship onto float trucks and drove off. A wall came down. We can't get back into the ship."

A murder cat leaped next to her and placed a paw on her hand.

"Me Mitsssy, Mother of SSSlayersss. Your sssucker has pack hearing."

"Uh, this cat is Mitsy, Mother of Slayers. Velvet has good hearing, she said," Mimi said.

"We hunt," Misty said. All four cats disappeared.

"They are hunting. They're gone, but let's stay quiet. I think they will warn us if copper aliens come back into the storage area."

"I need a bathroom," Chloe said.

"We'll probably have to choose a shadowed spot," Acacia whispered.

"Ugh. In outer space with all this tech and I have to pee on the floor." Chloe grouched.

"I have to, also. Chloe, why don't we look around. Maybe there is a bathroom for the workers," Hannah said.

"Be careful," Acacia said.

"We will."

"Hey. I have a bag of kibble. I filled it just in case. It was in with the blankets." Acacia plopped down a bag that probably held a couple gallons of brown chunks.

"Bless you."

Mimi crushed one for Velvet.

Chloe and Hannah returned. "We found a small bathroom along the back wall, so at least we have water and a toilet. Much nicer than the Wormship." Chloe flopped down and grabbed big handful of kibble. After taking care of their needs they all tried to rest.

Mimi checked on the unconscious Valryssians. "That gas really knocked them out. They all seem to be breathing normally, though."

One of the cats checked on them frequently.

Mimi was thankful the gas hadn't affected humans the same way. They would have been helpless.

The cats took turns wandering off into the storage area, but Velvet curled up in the crook of Mimi's neck. She tried to stay awake to be on guard. Being kidnapped was exhausting. Not to mention the sore muscles she had from dragging Kyre.

Eventually she fell asleep, too. Kyre started to move, and Mimi woke with a start, heart pounding. A murder cat lifted its head and blinked at her.

Velvet continued to sleep, so she was reassured nothing alarming had happened.

Kyre's eyes opened. They flashed from one color to another for at least thirty seconds, like bizarre Christmas lights. Finally, they turned to the natural human hazel. Mimi wondered if the lights were part of his part-alien biology or added by some kind of surgical technology.

CHAPTER SIX

"Where are we? What happened?" Kyre had the presence of mind to speak softly.

"Your transport was captured by a big ship. They must have broken in, there was a small tube of gas under a chair. It put all of you to sleep, but didn't make us Earth people sleepy, though we could smell it. We managed to hide you, the three children and all your cats in the luggage area below," Mimi explained. Acacia was awake, but Hannah and the children were still asleep, as were half the murder cats.

"The transport was dragged onto a huge silver ship. That big one with the golden trim that everybody was talking about when our worm kidnappers got smashed," Acacia said.

"We found a way to go through a little door on the floor to the ground below. The ship was parked near a storage area with lots of containers. We dragged everybody over here and hid. Soon after, a wall came down and blocked off the ship," Mimi continued.

Kyre sat up and checked the children. "They have less mass, so they might sleep a long time. That's probably good, they would all be frightened."

"We don't have any water, but we know where there's a restroom with water. Acacia has some of that kibble in our bag, so we have something to eat," Mimi said.

Kyre snapped his fingers, and the cats soon appeared on silent feet. "I'm going to send the cats out on patrol. They're going to send me images. I won't be able to talk for a little while." His eyes turned into yellow lights.

The cats took off, slinking around and jumping on top of containers. Kyre scooted so his back was to a container and sat there with his yellow-lit eyes half closed for some time.

He sat up. "The cats will return in a short while. No one is in the dock area right now, so we can move around a little. They assured me there is prey down here, probably crabrats, so they can find food. Do you still have your little nanosnoot?"

"Yes, she's here in my pocket," Mimi said.

"The cats can tell her if someone is about. We're going to have to find a way out of here, but right now we need somewhere better to hide, especially when the children wake."

He stood up and stretched. Mimi couldn't stop her sudden interest. He was well-built, wide of shoulder, narrow of abdomen, long legs with muscled thighs. She mentally slapped herself.

"I'm going to do some exploring. If you think there's any trouble or my little brothers and sister wake, have your nanosnoot whistle."

"All right, I will try. I don't know how to make her whistle."

"Just give a little whistle yourself. She'll catch on."

Kyre was gone for a long time, though they didn't have a watch for time.

"I don't even want to know what crabrats are," Chloe said in grumpy voice.

Acacia whispered. "One person can't go off on their own. What if they get hurt?"

"I agree. I can almost communicate with the murder cats. Somehow Velvet helps."

"That's good."

Mimi was so relieved when Kyre returned along with two murder cats. Acacia heard him and opened her eyes, but Chloe and Hannah remained asleep.

"I know where they are holding my brothers and sister-in-law. They are still asleep, so they may have been given a second dose of the sleep gas."

"So what do we do?"

"I have a plan, but I need help." He paused. "Actually, I need Mimi and her nanosnoot for my plan, but first we need to move."

"We were just thinking that perhaps it would be best if we worked in teams, so no one is alone," Acacia said, her voice groggy.

He grabbed a handful of kibble and wrinkled his nose at the taste. "I agree. I want to move everyone into the maintenance passages. They are narrow utility areas, much safer than here. Here, we can be seen by anyone walking above on those catwalks." He gestured above them to narrow strips of grated metal around the perimeter of the storage bay. "Some bots are working in the passages, but I think I can program them to ignore us."

They woke Hannah and Chloe and got organized. Kyre carried two sleeping children over his shoulders. Mimi and Acacia took turns carrying the little girl. They followed him to a plain oval door that led to a passage, not quite high enough for the adults to stand, and narrow. It was dimly lit every few feet by a dull yellow light. Kyre closed and sealed the hatch.

"This ship is a modified Doona long hauler. Not too different from Red Haven, the main difference is in shape and size." Kyre grinned. "Meaning my family designed the ship. The engines, the power system, and the computer system are almost identical to Red Haven's. What we have to do is take over the Bridge controls." His teeth gleamed white in the dim light. "Of course, the Bridge is held by ship's officers. But there is a back-up console for the Bridge."

A small egg-shaped robot rolled down the hall. Kyre grabbed it, opened a small door in the back, and showed them the button to shut it down. "Do this when one comes by. They do have recording devices, and we don't want anyone to look at those. These robots do general cleaning and some maintenance. They alert the crew if there's anything major." He showed wires and chips and all manner of things inside the small robot. "Now see this wire that hooks to the large rectangle toward the back? Undo it, it leads to the visual elements in the front. That way, if it reactivates, we won't have to worry about it recording our presence."

Everyone had to shuffle around in the narrow space to see what he was talking about.

"You just take this little tool and snip the wire. Then you go back to the larger rectangle. See the shiny chip? That's memory. You take the same tool and break the rectangle." It cracked and crumbled like glass.

"Once you do that, the robot will just sit there. It won't have any orders to follow or way to record. I'm going to leave you with this tool."

"I wish we had a way to communicate," Acacia said. "Especially since you're going to be moving around the ship doing things."

Kyre looked thoughtful. "The cats can move between us and give some limited information."

"Yes, I heard from Mitsy, Mother of Slayers," Mimi said.

"Good." Kyre handed the small wire clippers to Acacia. "The cat will have to prick your skin, since its nanos work through blood. It won't damage you." He frowned. "Maybe the cats can set up a bond now, before we need to communicate. I'll take two, leave two here."

The cats split into two teams. One went to Acacia and pricked her with a paw on her forearm. The two cats got around to all the Earthlings.

"This is so cool," Chloe said after a minute. "I can hear him talk. Eenie, The Slasher."

"This is Meenie, The Bloody Claw."

The third cat was Miney, The Sudden Death. Earth names." Mimi said.

Kyre grinned. "Yes, our library has Earth entertainment recorded. Books, also, though those were harder to get in the past. Moe is on Red Haven. She is expecting a litter. Moe the Merciless," Kyre said. "She has long cat fur like her mom."

"So what is the plan?"Acacia asked.

Kyre sat for a moment. "I get my family members here to the passage. I'll have to turn off some bots and security viewers for that. After they are hidden, I'll lock the Bridge to my signature and send the ship into Fera legal space. Send out an alert there are slaves on board. Then we get everyone on our transport and head to Red Haven."

"That sounds like a good plan, but won't someone figure out that you're moving the ship to Fera and come find you?" Mimi asked.

"I can put the navigation system on a ten minute delay. Not sure they'll guess the Auxiliary Bridge, they might think someone on the Bridge is doing the move. I can change all the protocols, so only the Auxiliary Bridge controls the ship, with my code. The ship's crew would have hours of work before they could take back the controls."

"I might have to subdue a guard or two." One of the murder cats jumped on his lap and started hissing.

"Oh, you're right. I was not thinking of the murder cats. They can take out guards. Or help."

"So, I need Mimi and Velvet, because they have a strong bond. Nanosnoots are generally used to clean up infestations of nanobots, but they have other uses, too. It's just a matter of communicating with them. She might be able to take out a few important components for us."

"So Velvet has some kind of chip something in her brain?" asked Mimi.

"Yes, nanobots. They have many functions. I believe the Auxiliary Bridge is up on the next level. Let's go."

Mimi took off her baggy cloak. Underneath she was wearing a simple black tunic and trousers with boots from the broken crate. She put a couple handfuls of kibble in her pocket, just in case. "It'll be a lot easier to move like this."

"We'll leave Mitzy with you. She can scout and see if the way is safe to the bathroom. Our cats will communicate with her," Kyre told the other women.

With hugs for the others, Mimi followed Kyre and two cats through the maintenance passages. They met two bots as they moved through the passages. Kyre shut down one of them with a sharp tool, and then he had her shut down the other. "Practice is good."

They came to a tall ladder bolted to the ship's wall. "Here, you need to put one of these belts on so if you fall you won't kill yourself." They both put on a safety belt that hooked to a rod in the center of the ladder and started to climb.

Mimi found it tiring since she'd been cramped up in that cage for months, but she persevered. It didn't hurt that the view of Kyre climbing ahead of her was enticing.

It must be shock. So not the time to get all crazy about some guy.

"We're going to come out into the passage. I'm going to send the cats to look around."

The passage was empty, as was the office with the auxiliary bridge console. Kyre used tools from his belt to open the door panel and make changes. Soon they were inside a small room with two chairs and a large computer set up. Kyre got on the computer while Mimi stood with the door cracked open and watched the long hallway.

"I've shut down all the bots around the docking bays and on this floor and the floor where my family are being held. We won't have to worry about them recording anything. I will try to freeze all security feeds and alarms. Might need Velvet to help.

"If I shut security alarms and feeds first, no one will know we're in here."

"Alarms are down. Now for your little friend." Kyre went to the com and started flipping through screens, finally stopping on one.

She picked up Velvet and told her there was a task for her to do. She wasn't sure she actually had a mental bond with the tiny animal. "Make sure you stay safe and return to us in the hiding place in the maintenance passage."

Kyre unlatched a small port on the computer casing and held Velvet up to the small opening. Velvet stuck her trunk into the hole and wiggled all over for a minute. She sat down like a puppy and looked at Mimi. Mimi pulled out a kibble and crunched it up on the computer console. "Here is some kibble before you go. You might need something for energy."

Velvet gave a little chirp, and vacuumed up the kibble dust. She wiggled into the passage.

"It will take a while for a connection," Kyre said. "But she is made to connect with diagnostics. I can then divert her to a different system."

Connecting with Velvet took less time than she expected. There was a beep. The screen now showed a schematic screen and tiny, ghostly Velvet down in the corner. Kyre flipped through screens again until a new screen showed, but Velvet was still in the corner.

"Can't shut down security from here. Velvet will have to climb up through the system to the main bridge."

"Are they connected?"

"Yes, there are conduits through the walls and floors."

He used a stylus attached to the com to highlight a route. "I am making a path for Velvet to follow. She'll go through the computer, and find the Bridge Security control board. I'll set up a fake program. She'll shut down the main security system and my false system will fill all the screens."

Mimi told Velvet to follow the path Kyre made, which was highlighted on the computer screen. Mimi doubted that Velvet would understand, but to her surprise, Velvet turned down a passage and made her way to the highlighted path. Mimi kept her eyes on the screen. "Good job, little buddy. You found the right path!"

As they watched, Velvet began walking through the system. The schematic changed, showing a larger view instead of a close up. A tiny bright light moved slowly.

"It's going to take a couple hours for her to get there. We don't have to stare at the screen the whole time, we can take breaks. I suspect she knows her destination."

"It's a long way for a nanosnoot."

"It is, but she'll likely find nano particles on the way which will boost her energy.

"Can you make another path, so she can get back to the hiding place? I would hate to lose her."

"Sure." He drew with the stylus.

"I didn't know that she could squeeze down that tiny."

"I don't think they have actual hard bones. More like cartilage, but spongier. They weigh nothing at all."

Now he was standing close to her, and she realized he was quite a bit taller than she was. She barely reached his shoulder. His eyes were changing colors rapidly.

"Are your eyes how you were born or do you have some kind of electronics inside them?"

"My eyes are not entirely human, because my mother is Trengulu. She has the third eye. We are also part Krveshin, a race that you probably haven't seen. Rather human-like but with white crystalline skin and hair. White or light blue eyes. Some of my cousins are part Kulag, with the trunks. Many trading clans are mixed races."

"So the lights are normal. I do have enhancements, though. Around the age of four in my clan, we receive visual enhancements and connections to our ship's computer brains. I am now partially connected to this computer system because it is based on our ships built on Doona. I am compatible. I have a translator chip, also."

"What is this ship called?"

"The Shen Rick Vell. The Ever-Victorious Ones. I suggest we sit down here and try to get some rest."

Mimi told Velvet she was going to rest for a moment. *Velvet can you talk with Eenie, the cat in the office?* Immediately, Eenie walked up to her and tapped her forearm. For a brief moment, Mimi saw a metal conduit with cables, bright chips, and Velvet's front paws climbing the cables. "So smart," she murmured

***

Mimi woke on a hard metal floor. Light came from the computer console above her.

She wasn't that uncomfortable. Her head was on a gently rising chest, and one leg covered her companion, saving that leg from the hard metal floor.

He checked the computer. "She's making good progress."

"I wonder if the restroom is safe."

He changed the viewer to show the corridor. "No one is nearby."

She slipped out and used the restroom, taking the time for a two-minute shower.

She returned with her clothes clinging to her body, but she was sure she smelled much better.

Kyre ran down the hall, too.

"She's in the Bridge computer now," Kyre said when he came back. Velvet had broken through thick wire and now was working on a glowing rectangular chip.

"When she has destroyed that, we are on!"

"It seems to be taking a long time, though."

"It is a hard substance, similar to the hull coating. But she's making progress."

"I hope the others are all right."

He nodded and looked off into space for a moment. "Mitsy says the kits are still sleeping." He patted her leg. "Your friends can communicate with the cats. Some part of the translator chips are working. The cats told them you are fine, and our plan is going well."

While they watched, another tiny nanosnoot joined Velvet. The two wrapped their trunks together for a moment, and soon the other small snoot joined her in breaking the chip.

"Oh, that's a relief," Mimi said. "Velvet has help now. This is taking so long."

"Computer system changes always take longer than you think. We still have some time. Probably about an hour. A Terran hour."

Mimi sat down on the floor and stretched out her legs. "A bit sore with all this exercise," she said.

He sat down next to her again.

"Want a shoulder rub?" He asked.

"Oh yes."

His hands were strong and pleasantly warm. Mimi couldn't help but notice he smelled nice, and his hair was damp from a quick shower also. "So tell me about your life on Red Haven."

"I work on board the ship on the bridge as Bridge Crew. I'm the First Officer, so do a little of everything. Mostly problem solving. Before I was First Officer I was a payload specialist, calculating the weight of our trades and sales, fuel calculations. Important job, but not very exciting."

"Sounds like a lot of math."

"Yes. Space traders need to be good at math, to make a profit. I also teach mathematics to children age ten to twelve. Teaching a few hours a week is an important service to our society, so many of us take on a part time course. We find that if children have a good foundation at that age, it is much easier for them to move into the higher calculations that are necessary for so many needs on a spaceship."

Mimi shook her head. "In this space world my friends and I are like primitives coming out of the woods. But I do like math. My schooling is in accounting. Business math. Profit, loss...."

Kyre raised his eyebrows. "That type of work is important on a trade ship. You can take courses to learn our computer systems, and fill in the gaps of your education. All people aboard the Havens have the right to education just like other essentials, like housing, good food, medical care."

"You are far more advanced in your society than we are on Earth." She was feeling warm and a bit too relaxed. His hands sent warmth deep into her muscles. It was the best thing she'd felt in ages. Before the worms.

"Perhaps." He shifted a bit, uncomfortably. "But we still have arranged marriages for many of our people. That's not advanced."

She wrinkled her nose. "Sounds awful to me."

CHAPTER SEVEN

Mimi was glad she'd taken a quick shower. Vain, no doubt. She didn't want Kyre to think she smelled bad. She was now sitting between his legs, leaning back against his chest while he massaged her upper arms.

Kyre had returned from the restroom with damp hair. Maybe he didn't want to stink to her, either. He got up and checked the computer again. She sighed, the magic fingers were now over. "Velvet and her new friend have broken through and are destroying individual filaments."

"Now we wait."

She nodded. "That's not a bad thing, though. With all the escaping and stress. I'm getting my strength back for the next burst of energy."

They sat quietly in the dim light of the console.

"So, are you pair bonded?" he asked

"Pair bonded? Like married?"

"Or betrothed or declared. In the clans, you can be married and not pair bonded."

"That doesn't sound great."

"It is often a lonely match, more like a business merger. My parents do not believe in arranged marriages. It is changing now, though our clan, but the Trengulu people are more traditional. Our strongest alliance is with them. Many couples declare their union before the clan at out Gathering Feast."

"What's that?"

"A couple stands before their family, usually dressed in matching colors, as a symbol of their union. They declare their intent to remain together until the next Gathering. They exchange worthy gifts. Then, when the clan gathers again in a few years, they sign contracts, or part. They keep the gift."

"So your brother who is married, he had a choice?" Kyre was sitting so close she could feel the heat of his body.

"Yes. They met as children and always cared for each other. I think his twin will Declare with Zhuzhana's sister soon, at the Gathering of Havens this annum."

"Is that like a meeting?"

"Yes. Every three years, annums, we call them, all the Havens meet in a secret location in space. It is a time of business meetings, a huge combined market, and also marriages and celebrations. Much frivolity."

"Sounds like fun. How many Havens are there?"

"Fifteen Havens. Magenta Haven is the newest. Many of Red Haven's people moved there, to give it a start. Then there are all types of smaller ships, family traders, contracted crew ships. They also join us."

He was silent for a while. He shifted his legs and they brushed hers.

I want to kiss him. Not pair bond or anything serious. Just a little pleasure.

"Do your people have rules? Like making people marry if they ...you know?"

He frowned at her. "You know what?"

"Um. Making out. Sex."

He shifted. "Well, a child together can force a marriage, or a contract concerning the life of the child."

"But what if the couple just has a fling?"

She was shocked at her own boldness. She'd French kissed a guy on St Patrick's Day at a bar, but hadn't been involved with anyone since she was nineteen.

"No. Couples can be together, physically. Even some marriage contracts allow pleasure mates." He looked at her. His hand trailed down her hair to her nape, making her shiver. "You are very pretty, so many will want pleasure with you. Of course, our medics will have to find a way to control fertility. Unless you want to have a baby."

She had a sudden vision of a tiny child with dark curls and hazel eyes. "Oh! No. Someday. But I don't want a baby now. I'd like to be, uh, pair bonded first."

"Me, also." His hand reached up and stroked her cheek. "Though a brief time of pleasure would be wonderful."

Her breath vanished, "Oh. Um, yes. No baby making, though."

He grinned. "Of course. I am responsible. I have my fertility halted at this time."

He brushed his fingers over her lips. "Do you kiss? My family kisses. Some Trengulu clans think it strange."

"Yes. I kiss." She could barely talk, though. Her heart was racing, her breathing a bit shallow.

"Would you like to kiss for a while? A pleasant way to spend our time, yes? I have...been aware of you since we met."

She drew in a breath. "I've noticed you, too." She looked into his hazel eyes, noticing the patches and speckles of color as they caught the light from the console. "Kiss. Yes. "

Well, she sounded primitive. She blushed at her language failure.

He grinned. "I think kissing is moving pretty fast as it is."

She snorted and fingered his soft brown curls. "Yes, let's kiss a bit, alien man."

His lips were soft, his tongue seemed to know all her pleasure points. Delight zinged through her, causing her to make little noises in the back of her throat. The first kiss was followed by endless kisses. His fingers threaded through her hair, creating warmth through her whole body.

She swore his skin had to have some kind of magnet in it, because she didn't want to take her hands off him, once they slid up under his shirt. To her surprise, his nipples looked human but were a dark teal in color. He had a strong core, with defined abs. She kissed one, savoring the taste of his smooth skin.

He moaned as she kissed him and soon his hungry lips had her sports bra out of the way and eagerly found her nipple. His mouth was hotter than she expected, tongue softer. Molten blood ran through her veins, waking every inch of her body, her core, making her moan.

Some sexy alien quality.

Soon she was on her back, and he was half over her. Pressed together so tight, she knew he had human-like male anatomy.

A loud murder cat yowl and paw smack on Kyre's forehead dragged them out of their obsession with the flesh.

"Oh. Right." He leaped up to the console.

"Filaments are cut, chip is disabled," he said, his mouth in crooked grin. "Good timing, I guess. Or maybe bad."

Mimi got up and stood beside him, their hands entwined for a moment, and then he got busy on the console.

He slid a glance at her and grinned. "I can't believe we were so involved when we just met. No one would believe it."

She snorted. "Acacia would. She saw me look at you when you woke. You stretched."

He grinned. "Which one is Acacia again?"

She was inordinately pleased he hadn't really noticed the other women. "She's the one with dark curly hair and brown skin. Tall, round."

"Not the child."

"No, that's Chloe. And the light-haired woman is Hannah."

While they chatted, his fingers continued to work the console. At one point he leaned over the console and a light shined in one eye.

"We're in. The slave room is keyed to only my retina."

He grabbed her hand, and they rushed though the halls, up several access stairs until they came to a long, empty passage. Honestly it looked exactly like all the other passages. Mimi was glad he was finding their way, because she was lost.

On the way to the slave room they found a small float hauler. Kyre got it started and made sure she could start it to, with a bit of work on the computer panel. When they got to the door, Kyre had his retina scanned and the door popped open. They entered a room full of people asleep on narrow beds, hooked to fluids and monitor machines. Kyre sighed. "We will have to find clothing. They are set up for long-term sleep." Then he made a funny little gasp and slumped to the floor with a thud.

Mimi stared at his unconscious form for a moment, too shocked to move. "Holy crap! Crapity crap crap crap!"

She groaned. "How did we not think of this?" Leaning over, she grabbed Kyre's legs to pull him out of the room full of sleeping gas. She groaned as she tried to move him. "Still heavy."

Movement out of the corner of her eye got her attention. A man sat up. He had dark brown skin with very short dark curls, and massive muscled shoulders. To Mimi, he looked like an African American. But, of course, that was back home in Wichita, not here in outer space. He was probably some kind of alien.

"You spoke English," he said.

She stared at him in shock for a moment. "You're from Earth?" she asked.

"Oklahoma," he said.

Mimi blinked at him. "Go Sooners," she said weakly. "I'm from Wichita. I need to get this man out of here. He's part alien, and the gas in here got to him." She pulled, making little progress. "He is so heavy. Alien heavy. Oh my God, Kyre, are your bones made of lead?"

"Do you work on this ship?" the human asked. "I've only seen robots. I'm Grady McCall. Gunnery sergeant, United States Marine Corps. Call me Grady."

"No, we were in a small transport ship headed to Kyre's homeship. These slavers filled the ship with gas, and all the alien family passed out. Then they dragged our ship into a docking bay using robot arms."

"But you didn't fall asleep because you're from Earth."

"Right. Kyre's twin brothers and sister-in-law are in this room with you. We came to get them and hopefully get away on our transport ship."

"Take me with you. I can be pretty handy. I've been pretending to be asleep for days."

"Sure."

The man took off his IV tubes and got out of the bed with the sheet around him. He pulled open a drawer underneath and pulled out clothing. It wasn't long before he was dressed in desert camo, down to combat boots.

"So you were abducted too?" Mimi asked.

"Yes. I woke up in bed, hooked up with IVs of some type. There were all these others, but they were asleep. I knew they weren't human. A number of the women have three eyes. One guy has an elephant trunk."

"Kyre, my friend here, his family married into a clan of the three-eyed people. He's also part human. But he weighs a ton."

The man grabbed Kyre by the legs and pulled him out into the hallway.

"Thanks," Mimi said. "I'm Mimi Stevens, college student from Wichita. This is Kyre Valryssian, a space trader. Some human ancestry. Oh, we can't let the door close. It needs Kyre's retina to open," she said.

Grady went to his bed and brought a wad of tape from his IV's. He taped around the door latch. "See if this works," he said, shutting himself in the hallway with her inside the room. He was able to open the door with his fingernails in the crack. "Works."

"Now what? We need to get out of here. What was your plan?"

"Load his brothers and sister-in-law on that float hauler, and take them to our hiding place," Mimi said. "Then get on our ship and get away. We have already changed the navigation so this ship will move into space where slavery is illegal."

Grady dressed the two men while Mimi struggled to get clothes on the woman. Mimi doubted she would have been able to lift even one of them onto the hauler. Good thing she'd met Grady.

Kyre was waking a little now and had sat up while Grady was still loading his relatives.

"The room was full of sleeping gas," Mimi told him.

He made a disgusted face. "Didn't think of that."

"Can't think of everything, I guess," she said.

Kyre stared at the very tall, broad marine.

"This is Kyre Valryssian, part Earth-man, part alien space trader. He rescued my friends and me." Mimi frowned. "I guess now we rescued him back. This is Grady McCall, US Marine Corps. Earth military, the tough kind. He's going to help us."

"Thanks," Kyre said. "Plenty of room for you on Red Haven."

"That's his big ship," Mimi explained. "Like a mother ship."

Kyre explained how to drive the hauler and Grady took the controls. They headed for a lift.

"What are those cat things?" Grady asked. The murder cats leaped onto the hauler as it floated away.

"Part cat from Earth, mixed with a predator from planet called Doona. Psychic," Mimi said.

Grady frowned.

Mimi explained further while Kyre slumped over, asleep again. "They prick your skin with a claw, and you can communicate with them in your brain. There's another animal that does that, too. A tiny one." She frowned. "I hope my Velvet comes back."

She turned to the cats. "Hey, can you tell my little nanosnoot to go to the hiding place? Or help her get there?" One cat leaped off the hauler and slunk away.

Then she turned to Kyre, who was dozing again. "I'll have to wake him. I don't know how to get to the hiding place from here." She patted his face.

"Yes. Yes, I'm awake." He still sounded like a sleep talker and his eyes were still closed. Mimi snorted and patted harder.

One of the cats leaped over to Kyre and smacked him on the cheek, leaving six pinpricks from his claws.

Kyre's eyes opened and patted the cat. "I needed that, Eenie."

"Could the cats scout ahead?" Grady asked. "Do they have that capability?"

"Yes. Good idea. Pack, can you connect with Grady here?" The cats leaped near the Marine. "It will only be a little prick."

The cats stretched out their claws and connected. "Wow," Grady said after a minute. "Alien cats."

"We are going down this hall and turning left. There's a lift," Kyre said. Mimi rubbed his shoulders to try to keep him awake.

The cats ran off. They started on the floor, but then walked up the metal walls.

"How do they do that?" Mimi asked, shocked.

Kyre shrugged. "Some magnetic enhancement. Not sure, to be honest. My cousin is always trying different things on them. New abilities."

They hurried through the corridors and got on the lift. When it stopped, the cats slipped out to scout.

"Two men at the end of the hall, where it intersects another," Grady whispered. "What are the white sticks they're holding?"

"Weapons. They can stun, stun and incapacitate, or kill."

Grady nodded. He seemed to be deep in thought.

"Stay here and stay quiet. The cats are causing a distraction for me."

For such a huge man, Grady moved light on his feet. He returned with the cats, dragging two men in gray uniforms. Tube weapons were slung over his shoulder by straps. "Clear to the end of the hall."

He hoisted the two men into the trolley and proceeded to tie them up with torn cloth from the Zuzhanna's ruffled skirt. "Didn't want to leave them behind to alert anyone. We can find some place to stash them. I, uh, incapacitated them."

With the cats running ahead, they made their way through empty corridors to a second lift, and finally to a long hallway with a wall hatch. From that point, they couldn't use the trolley. Kyre managed to drag one brother while Grady dragged the other two with Mimi's help.

Grady also brought the guards into the passage. "Show me how to use this." He held the tube weapon.

"Small button, stun. Mid-sized button, incapacitate. Large button, kill," Kyre said.

McCall zapped the two men. "Incapacitated it is."

They got to the others, and Kyre slid down to the floor, yawning.

"Hey, everyone," Mimi said. "This is Sergeant Grady McCall from Oklahoma. United States Marine. He was in the sleeper room with lots of other abducted people, but the gas didn't make him sleep."

"I think I need to rest a little." Kyre said. "Sorry, everybody."

Mimi patted his shoulder. "Get some rest."

Kyre stretched out and went to sleep.

"The gas in the room where they were holding the others knocked Kyre out," Mimi said. "I was lucky Sergeant McCall was there and awake. I couldn't have moved Kyre or the other three very far."

"Hello ladies," Grady smiled at the women.

For an older man with a touch of gray, he was pretty attractive. Mimi gave Acacia a *look*. Acacia rolled her eyes at Mimi.

"This is Hannah, Acacia, and Chloe. We were all abducted at the same time and place from Wichita. By spaceworms that stunk."

"Wow. Please call me Grady," said the sergeant. He held out his hand for a shake. "So what's the plan for getting away from here?"

"The transport ship isn't far from here. It's near a storage area with many crates and containers. Good for hiding."

"Storage containers are my life," Chloe grumbled.

Acacia nodded. "This is the second time since we were abducted that we got away and hid in a storage area."

"After Kyre woke up from the gas in the transport, we found a console that has the same functions as the Bridge," Mimi said. "Kyre's family builds ships, and this ship is one they built.

That made Grady grin.

"He shut down security alarms and cameras. We had a little tiny animal called a nanosnoot. It's made in a lab for cleaning computer equipment of invasive nanos. Kyre directed her around electronics inside computers and stuff, so he could take over. It's hard to explain."

Grady raised his eyebrows and nodded.

"Anyway, our plan is to get on the transport and get away with Kyre flying it, since his brothers would be asleep. But now Kyre's kind of sleepy, so I guess we'll just wait here until everybody wakes up."

"Those alien cats are pretty handy," Grady said.

"We've been calling them murder cats because, look at their claws," Chloe said, holding up one of the cat paws with inch-long claws. "It's weird when they talk in your mind."

"Did Velvet make it back?" Mimi asked. "We told her to come back to the hiding place. One of the cats went looking for her."

Chloe shook her head and looked quite sad. "No, we haven't seen her. I hope she makes it back. I'd hate to leave her here on this ship."

"We have some food if you're hungry," Acacia said to Grady, holding out her bag of kibble. "It's not good food, it's like dog kibble. But it's not poisonous. We've been eating it for months."

After a while, Mimi showed Grady where the restroom was. She pointed out the wall that hid the transport. "That wall moves up, and our ship is on the other side of it."

Back in the hiding place, they went to sleep.

CHAPTER EIGHT

Mimi woke to a gentle tapping on her cheek. She opened her eyes to see Velvet had returned. "Oh, sweetie, I'm so glad you're back," she whispered.

"Not only Velvet, but lots of other nanosnoots," Acacia said. Her arm was covered in snoots in various shades of soft colors, sage, heather, lavender, silver, mauve. Three were the size of Velvet, but at least a dozen tiny snoots with fluffier hair, the size of her thumbnail, wiggled around.

"Babies!" Chloe squealed.

The other three children woke up. "I'll take them to the bathroom," Chloe said. "But don't worry, a cat will check it out for me." Hannah left with the children, and when they returned, the children industriously crushed kibble to feed the snoots. Babies crawled all over them, to their delight.

"This is the best abduction ever," Chloe quipped to a tiny mauve baby.

There was an odd growling, whining sound Mimi hadn't heard before, running constantly in the background. She wondered how long Kyre had been asleep. Maybe he could wake up and fly the transport.

"Kyre can you wake up? Are you feeling better?" Kyre sat up, and his eyes went through that alien flashing that they had done before.

Grady sat up. He now had six tubes slung over his shoulder.

"Grady, what happened? Where did you get all the weapons?" Mimi asked.

"Oh. Everyone went to sleep, but I wasn't tired, so I went hunting. I thought it might be a good idea to fill those four empty beds in the slave room." He grinned. "No one removed my tape from the door. The beds are full now. I even stuck in the IVs. I restunned the two at the other end of this passage."

He patted the tubes. "I like these. So light weight. Accurate, too. The cats were a big help. One disappeared and returned covered in those little mousy things, but I figured that was the animal you were talking about."

He paused and frowned. "What's the deal with his eyes?" He waved toward Kyre.

"I'm not sure. They are all part alien. With enhancements," Mimi said.

"Sergeant, would you like some kibble?" Acacia asked.

"Oh no," Kyre said, leaping up. "They've turned on the jump drive."

"What does that mean?" Grady asked.

"The engines have to warm up before they make a long-distance jump, and they've turned them on to warm. That whining sound will go away when the engines are ready. We still have a chance to stop them." Kyre ran a hand through his hair.

"If they jump, getting in the transport's not going to do any good. We'll be somewhere unknown, and the transport is not made for long distances."

"So what are we going to do?" Hannah sounded strained.

Kyre looked around. "Well, my brothers aren't going to be any help." His gaze turned to Grady. "Where did you get all those weapons?"

"While you all slept, the cats and I went hunting. Now there are bodies in those empty beds. Maybe the robots won't notice some of us escaped."

"I hadn't thought of that," Kyre admitted. "The robots probably do send an alarm if someone is missing. Thanks."

"I know nothing about your equipment, but I'm very good at combat," Grady said.

"Here, have some kibble," Acacia said, holding the bag out to Kyre, who threw a handful into his mouth.

"Where did all these snoots come from?" Kyre grabbed another handful of kibble.

"They returned with Velvet," Mimi said.

Kyre nodded. "Maybe they can help." He waved a hand toward Grady. "I believe they could come in handy. I need to get back to the bridge console. Grady, will you come with me? Let me see if I can get the adult snoots to help." He put a hand on one cat's head. He was quiet for a while.

"Children, can you keep track of all the babies while I take the adults to Engineering? Make sure to count them." The children were thrilled with this task.

"We're going to take the adult snoots and two of the cats with us. Grady will be handy if we run into personnel," Kyre said. "I need to go to the Auxiliary Bridge and then probably to Engineering. Mimi, I'm leaving three shooters with you."

He explained how they worked.

"Do incapacitate," Grady said. "You do not want the aliens waking up on you. We are in hostile territory."

***

Waiting was nerve wracking. The women made sure everyone ate something, and took silent trips to the restroom when the cats told them it was clear.

"I hope we can get away," said Acacia.

"It seems to be taking a long time," Hannah whispered.

Mimi stretched out and covered her eyes with her forearm. So much had happened in the last day. *The Valryssians, Kyre and his smooth, sweet kisses. Murder cats, slaves. Grady.* She suspected her pulse was racing because she couldn't calm down. She dozed fitfully. Whenever anyone moved, her eyes flew open.

"Kyre seems to know what he's doing. And Grady is scary competent," Acacia said, patting her arm. Hannah nodded.

The children played happily with the baby snoots.

What a time to find an intriguing man. Mimi relived their time together, analyzed what he told her about his life. Remembered the kissing.

The whine stopped.

"I think they did it," she whispered. "Kyre said that whine was the engines warming up."

"Children, why don't you try to tell the baby snoots they need to go into your pockets or Chloe's bag, because we need to move soon," Acacia said. The children did so, counting the little puffs over and over to make sure they weren't missing any.

Finally, Mimi heard movement down the long passage. The two cats, with the adult snoots riding on their backs, arrived first, followed by the men.

"The jump engines are down. Multiple hydraulic leaks throughout the system."

Kyre and Grady grinned. Grady had even more weapons. "Also, their robotic arms and weapon systems are offline. I changed the passwords and sequences. It'll take them hours to fix everything."

"So what do we do now?" Mimi asked.

"Now we go back to our original plan. We haven't changed position, they were just warming up their engines. There are workers about now, so we will have to be careful."

"Leave them to me," Grady said. "Cats, come with me."

All four cats rubbed against him and left with him. "I think he is one of their pack, now," Kyre said. We'll wait for him to report."

Grady returned some time later. "I incapacitated eight men. Workers, not guards."

"Time to go." Kyre grabbed one of his brothers and dragged him to the container area. Mimi and Acacia teamed up on the sister-in-law, while Grady brought the other brother.

"Zhuzhana. I finally remembered her name," Acacia whispered. While they were getting the sleepers out, Hannah brought the children, who waited quietly in the shadows. Kyre managed the panel. "We have to wait for the light to change to blue. Our level of breathable air."

While they waited, the cats leaped on top of containers and kept watch.

"Now." Kyre rushed and opened the wall, then opened the ship. The children scurried across with Chloe in the lead. The rest of them dragged the heavy sleepers to the transport. They wrestled the Valryssians into the seats.

"I'll leave you to get everyone harnessed. Fast." Kyre said and went to the pilot controls.

The three Earth women got everyone harnessed. Grady came in last.

"I feel like I'm going to faint," Acacia said.

"Deep breaths, everyone," Grady said.

The ship launched smoothly out into space. Kyre didn't turn on the view screen on the wall, but maybe they didn't need to see if the alien ship was firing on them. Mimi searched for gas hisses.

"We're good." Kyre said over a speaker. "I have on a helmet and am breathing container air, just in case they try the gas weapon again. Their weapons can't harm our hull. I'm contacting Red Haven. They'll send an escort."

A few minutes later, the view screen turned on. "We should be able to see the escort soon. The Shens have sent out a security ship, but it is not as fast as we are. Haven Strikers will be here in moments. Fast, two-man combat ships."

Grady leaned forward. "I want to see those."

On the screen, lights blinked. The three Valryssian children cheered. "There they are," Kyre said.

Soon slim silver ships joined them. "Kind of star-shaped," Mimi said.

"Those are astroid shaped, a curved four point star. I learned that in math," Chloe said. "We did mathematical shaped art."

A boxy ship fired at them from a distance. The smaller ships zipped off to confront the boxier ship, firing and twirling about. Definitely alien, Mimi thought.

Two larger ships, surrounded by more Strikers, joined them. "Fera Space Guard. We sold them scores of strikers ships," Kyre said.

These Strikers were dark gray with bright green and purple markings. "The big ships are Border Patrol, from Fera, weaponized. They have suction locks. They can blast a hole in a ship, suction around it and board through the lock. The slave ship is navigating into Fera territorial space. Against their will, I might add." Kyre laughed.

Grady gave a whoop.

Soon they could see Grzbt and beyond it, the planet Fera. "We are going on to Red Haven," Kyre said.

They passed the planet and in the distance was a glowing ruby red saucer ship. "It looks like a jewel" Mimi said, surprised.

"Yes, that is our latest hull technology, a type of crystal. The coloring is actually done with lights. We can turn them off if we want," Kyre replied. "You'll find the clan is fond of colored lights."

Mimi grinned, thinking of his flashing eyes.

In the distance, they could see bright flashing lights on the zephyr's hoods.

"Border Patrol will board the Shen ship, treating them as a hostile. They'd be smart to surrender," Kyre said. "Fera has a strong Border Patrol in order to maintain their reputation as a prime tourist and luxury destination. They will take care of the captives on Fera."

Mimi relaxed a bit hearing that. The white hats were on it.

"It's so pretty," Chloe said as they neared Red Haven.

"Hull composition is crucial in space. Ours is a family secret, though we do sell a few ships with our hulls and offer the technology to buyers."

"The hulls protect you from radiation?" Acacia asked.

"Yes. We have been able to protect our people from radiation for many generations, but the hulls were extremely thick and high maintenance. Our new hulls are stronger and thinner."

"You live on the ships full time?" Mimi asked.

"Some clan members live on planets or stations along our trade routes. My family lives on Havens. They are like cities, with schools, restaurants, entertainment, apartments, and green spaces."

The transport landed inside the enormous ship, and some type of suction connectors sealed over their door and opened to a walkway. Medics with patient floaters waited to collect the sleepers.

Mimi followed the others to a long hallway with many lift tubes. "The tubes go in different directions. Our housing areas are color coded green," Kyre said. "I'll be taking you to empty rooms near my own apartment."

The tube had simple seats against the wall, and no windows. It took them up but also turned corners.

"We are going to a family residential area. There is a residential area close to the Bridge for the Captain and Bridge crew, but I like this area better. It has a nice walking path, play and exercise areas, and a green space. It is not very populated yet. This is the newest residential area opened up. There's also a small medical unit in case you hurt yourself," said Kyre.

"What about meals? Do we cook our own?" Acacia asked.

"You can if you wish," said Kyre. "There's also a residential cafeteria open all day. The menu is prepared by the ship's AI. I actually prefer that. It's quicker with no cleanup."

"That's probably what we'll do for a while," Mimi said. "Someone will have to show us how to use all the devices on the ship"

"You will have an AI tutor in your living quarters. Of course, my family and I will be available to answer questions. The first thing we need to do with you is get your language and visual chips updated. Our family does speak English and German, but on board the ship we generally speak Alliance Standard. The trade language."

"I would like to see something like a map or diagram of the ship and where everything is placed," Acacia said. "Just for my own knowledge. I won't go wandering around and causing trouble."

Kyre smiled. "I will make sure you have a full tutorial on the ship and how it functions. I think you will find it interesting."

"On Earth there is a type of fiction called science fiction which is all about people living in space and having exciting adventures. Acacia is quite a fan," Mimi said with a grin at her friend.

"We have a large library full of all types of stories, fiction, theater and music productions. Some are from Earth. Once your translator and visual chips work correctly, you will have access."

The lift came to a halt and the door swooped open. They stepped out onto a wide walkway. The whole area was open, with a high ceiling. "As you can see, there's a green space. It is also part of our air quality system. All the apartments border it. The cafeteria is the big pavilion in the middle."

An oval-shaped green park filled the area, with the apartments, six stories high, overlooking it.

Everything was made of a white material, like ceramic. All the apartments had balconies and large windows. They followed Kyre along the path on the side opposite the Green Space. Mimi could now see a pool and stream, seating areas under trees with trailing leaves, children's play equipment.

"You have a choice, because many units are still empty. You can choose any floor you want. There are lifts to the higher floors, of course. I am on the top floor, because I like the view. All rooms in the house overlook the park, so each of you will have a bedroom and a personal space."

"Do we all live together in one apartment?" Mimi asked.

"Most units have two bedrooms," Kyre said. "There are larger units, and they are generally on the first and second floor. We have found that children have a tendency that throw things off of balconies, so we try to confine them to the lower floors."

Acacia put an arm around Chloe. "I think you should live with me. But I'll let you choose the apartment."

"That's a great idea," Mimi said. Acacia was motherly, and probably far more mature than Mimi or Hannah.

But then that left her with Hannah. They got a long better now, but she didn't really want to live with her.

Chloe squealed in delight. "Top floor!"

"You're not going to chuck things off the balcony, are you?" Kyre teased.

Chloe rolled her eyes. "Not unless you make me really mad and then run away. I might try to nail you with something."

He laughed. "You remind me of my sister."

"All single adults can have their own unit," Kyre said as they walked through the sixth-floor unit Chloe picked. He moved close to Mimi and once again her skin wanted to meld with his.

Definitely some magnetic alien thing going on.

"There is a unit right next door to me. We could get to know each other." His hazel eyes searched hers.

"I guess if we dislike being neighbors, I could move."

"Easily."

"I'll take a unit close to Chloe and Acacia. That way we're all on the sixth floor," Hannah said.

"I'm not one for heights," Grady said. "Is there a small unit on the ground level?"

They found Grady an apartment on the first floor.

"I'm going to set the doors up so that the door lock recognizes you and lets you in. Just a thumb scan." Kyre tapped on the door panel.

Grady was soon settled in a place right across from the park. "If no one needs me, I think I'll get some rest."

"When you wake, check your doorstep. A servobot should bring a bag of clothing. I'll pick you up in three hours for a meal," Kyre said.

The rooms were comfortable with padded sofas and chairs in neutral colors. The small kitchen and combined living room opened up to the balcony. There was no glass in the window, it was all open.

"So everything's temperature-controlled, and there's no rain?" Acacia asked.

"The lower floors have glass because of the sprinkler system in the park, but the droplets don't reach up here. You'll hear two bells when it turns on."

The bedrooms were large, containing a double sized bed and bathroom to the side. They all had different colored tiles in the bathrooms and kitchens. Hannah was delighted hers was yellow. Acacia's and Chloe's tile was light blue and Mimi's was mauve.

Acacia said, "Set ours up so Mimi and Hannah can come in whenever they want. That way we can visit and help each other out. I know I'm going to want to cook nice dinners in my own place sometimes."

"I can't believe we are going to live in these pretty apartments. After the cage!" Mimi said.

Hannah nodded. "I have a lot to be thankful for."

"I will leave you to get settled, but I will return to take you to the cafeteria," Kyre said. "Push the blue button on the door panel if you need anything. Your clothes should be here soon."

Mimi walked down the hallway with Kyre to her own apartment.

"I'll gather everyone for a meal. After our meal, would you like to walk in the park?"

"I'd like that." The way her heart jumped, she'd *really* like that. Maybe they would kiss again.

"Tomorrow will be a busy day. We'll upgrade your chips and set up AI bots for your apartments. They are helpful and can teach you how to use the tech around here. Eventually you'll have your own holocom armband. Until then, Zhuzhana and I will check with you several times a day." He pressed a kiss on her lips.

"Now I must report to Captain Rhodes. He'll make me see the medic." He made a face.

Mimi grinned, then thought of something. "Will we hear about the slavers?"

"Fera Border Patrol is investigating. They may want to interview you. We will be informed of the findings."

"Great."

Mimi wandered around her apartment and then walked down to Acacia's.

"There are drinks in the refrigerator," Chloe said from her place on a cushioned balcony swing where she was playing with baby snoots.

Hannah stepped in. "I'm going to take a long shower and then a nap. I had all of you keyed into my place if there is ever a problem."

"Super. Get some rest."

"I think I'm going to do the same," Acacia said. "Chloe, you can wake me up if you need me."

"I think I'm good. I'll shower in a little while. Wonder what kind of clothes we'll get?" Chloe was playing with two baby snoots, one silver and one mauve, while a dusty pink adult wandered around the balcony. "I get to keep these snoots, Mimi. All the kids got some."

Mimi grinned. "That's pretty cool."

"The other kids and I are going to build them habitats in life science class. I get to join in as soon as my translator works. They are made so the adult snoots can take off to clean bad nanos sometimes."

"It's an important job."

She sat in the kitchen area with Acacia and they shared a bottled tea type drink.

"Chloe is adapting so quickly. She's looking forward to everything," Acacia said.

"That's a relief."

"I admit, I am feeling totally overwhelmed," Acacia said. "Relieved, but still...jumpy. Wishing this was Long Island Iced Tea."

Mimi laughed. "You know, I thought you'd be stuffy. Like Hannah."

"Honestly, Mimi, stereotypes!" Acacia frowned at her.

"Yeah, I know. I'm trying to grow as a person." She sipped her tea. "I've seen Hannah really warm up to Chloe."

"Hannah is introverted, a perfectionist, and likes a strict routine. You can see how this abduction was harder on her than the rest of us," Acacia said, too low for Chloe to overhear. "Her mother was something else, may she rest in peace."

Mimi decided to change the subject. She still wanted to spend some time thinking. A journal would be helpful. She'd ask Kyre. "Long Island Iced Tea sounds good. I bet we could make a lot of money running a little cocktail bar."

Acacia made a face. "I, for one, am not interested in tending bar. We'll get an aptitude test. I'm excited to see what type of careers I might qualify for. What if I could work on the Bridge?"

Mimi laughed. "The Holy Grail of Jobs!"

They were silent for bit, sipping the drinks.

"One huge change after another," Mimi said, feeling a bit overwhelmed. "But my accounting background will be helpful on a trader ship."

Acacia hummed and found another drink in the back and opened it. She grinned. "Not Long Island Iced Tea, but definitely a type of wine!"

Mimi grinned, and they spit the small bottle.

"Chloe?" Acacia called.

"Yeah?"

"You can't have any of these orange bottles, they are wine. There are five."

"Kay." She went back to whistling to the babies, who whistled back.

"Do you think Kyre has some type of magnetic quality? Alien quality?" Mimi asked.

"Why do you ask?"

She lowered her voice. "My skin wants to glue itself to his."

Acacia laughed. "That could be plain, old-fashioned lust. He is a handsome man. Well, alien. And you've been stuck in a cage for months. Hormones out of control."

"His bones might be made of alien lead."

"True."

"Are your hormones out of control?" Mimi asked. "Grady is also quite handsome."

"I've always seen myself with someone more...scholarly. Not a military man of action. And I have spoken to him and feel no magnetic qualities."

"Yet."

Acacia rolled her eyes. "I'm going to take a very long shower, followed by a nap. This wine made me sleepy."

"Me, too."

***

Mimi left Acacia's apartment just as Kyre walked out of the lift. He saw her and smiled. She felt that the magnetic quality was in full force because she seemed to rush down the hallway to him. Colliding against him, their arms snapped tight around each other.

"I have the next three days off, so I can show you around the ship," Kyre said. "Rhodes thought that all of us involved in the abduction needed a few days off, even though the medic says we're just fine."

"I'm glad you're all fine, what with the sleeping gas and all."

"You will all be getting a check-up tomorrow. Would you like to join me in my apartment for a little while? We have several hours until dinner." His eyes searched hers.

Tingles swept through Mimi as she thought of some alone time with him.

"I would like that."

They hurried down the hall together, grinning like naughty children. They made it into his apartment, unseen. His arms closed tight around her, and he turned her until her back was against the door. Lips, soft but with enough pressure to open hers, pressed a deep, fervent kiss.

The kiss spread warmth straight to her core. Mimi threw her arms and legs around him.

"I'm on fertility controllers, so I can't get you pregnant. If we choose to do that," Kyre said. "Just so you know we're safe."

Mimi ran her hands through his silky hair and pressed kisses down his neck. His sweet spicy scent filled her, and she breathed him in. "Good to know," she said, her voice breathy.

He swung her around and carried her into his living room, to a couch with soft cushions in shades of green. They landed with a bounce, and he pushed her back against the arm. Velvet leaped off her shoulder and scampered to the balcony. Mimi snorted in amusement.

"We won't be interrupted here," he said. "Unless you want to be interrupted. I know this is moving pretty fast."

Mimi took a shaky breath. Not because she was scared on nervous. Because she was inflamed. Ravenous. Just being on the couch with him, his heavy chest pressed to hers, sent heat coursing through her veins.

She looked deep into his hazel eyes. "I don't feel like being cautious, or that I'm taking any kind of risk. I think being with you is a celebration. I lived through those worms and now, somehow, I'm in a good place. I want to experience all I can with you. Right now."

No point in being shy. Not when what I want is right here.

"You are in a good place." he groaned, the rasp of his voice sending goose bumps to her flesh. "With me."

He was ...luscious. Silken hair, smooth skin. Their lips collided, not gentle, but all pleasure. His tongue teased and thrust against hers, playing an intimate game that made her melt. Mimi wiggled until her legs were around his hips, pulling him close to her apex.

His heart pounded fast and hard against her chest, she could feel a thrusting rod against her thigh as they kissed. *He is as hungry as I am.* With a ragged breath she tugged at her tunic top and it came off over her head.

He hummed his pleasure at the exposed flesh. His hot, hard hands slid up her torso, working under her stretch bra and moving it up and off with her help.

"So, so pretty," he groaned against her breast, before taking a nipple. For a moment she couldn't move as pleasure strummed though her.

Mimi wanted him naked and grabbed his tunic, impatient to be flesh to flesh. Her toes slid into his waistband and yanked down at his leggings. He helped with one hand while his other cupped her breast, so he could continue feasting on her nipple. She wiggled out of her baggy pants with his help.

Finely, flesh to flesh. Heated skin molding to her own.

"Share pleasure?" His voice, low, sent a shiver of need through her.

"Yes. All of it." Her words made him shiver and she rejoiced in her power over his passions. They were equal in the overwhelming desire.

Had it always felt this good? Or was it part of his alien quality? Her heart pounded, the slickness between her legs pooled, she was so ready for him.

His turgid rod pressed her thigh, and Mimi maneuvered until it was where she wanted it, at her wet, throbbing nub. His weight grounded her to a safe place after floating like a free balloon pushed by the winds for so long. His throbbing heat against her most sensitive flesh held all her attention. His strength was bringing her closer, she was no longer wafting in the unknown. Now she was where she should be.

His finger stroked through her hair and his lips continued across her neck. Her skin felt heated wherever he touched. Each movement caused a slight press of his cock right where she wanted it. Anticipation made her breath heavy, noisy.

All her nerve endings tingled with pleasure. But still she wanted more. She slipped from anticipation to aching and tightened her legs around his hips. She wanted to feel the heat of him the strength deep inside.

His fingers gently slide between her legs and there was no hiding how wet and needy she was. Her hips thrust against his knowing fingers, as he circled and teased her most sensitive nub of desire.

He thrust his hard member against her thigh as he stroked her. "Out of control," he gasped.

Their skin was now slick with sweat, making every movement of their flesh a gliding caress, causing Mimi's breath to hitch.

His breath was loud, ragged.

It was music.

"I don't want to go slow," she said. "I want to ride the whirlwind and catch on fire with you. Combust."

Kyre raised up and looked deep into her eyes. "Sounds perfect to me."

He plunged into her, fast and deep. She cried out her approval, groaning in time with each thrust, reveling in his strength, his deep claiming. The whirlwind soared, winding her tighter and tighter, until she burst into a flame of pure pleasure.

Kyre followed her with a cry, joining her in heated pleasure.

They didn't move, breathing heavy.

"Wow," Mimi said. "No words."

He grinned, though his breathing was still harsh. "We do this often," he gasped. "My words."

"Oh, yeah," she moaned.

Mimi wondered how she would keep the others from knowing she'd just had the best sex of her life. More than sex. Something...profound. Crazy. Irresistible.

Now tired, they caressed gently without speaking, sometimes dozing. "We have to get ready," Kyre said reluctantly after they had enjoyed each other again, just as much, but slower. They showered together but had to rush.

"Come back to my place later, after dinner," Kyre insisted.

"Oh yes," she said, wrapping her arms around her.

He had his bot bring over her packet of new clothes. The clothing consisted of thigh-length tunics, long layered skirts and dresses, stretch leggings and soft boots. Stretchy underwear. Everything was stretchy. Mimi was content, since she lived in leggings and t-shirts back on Earth. The colors were darker hues, blues, greens and reds. She put on a wine red sleeveless dress with the long flounces, since they were going out to eat. Tan leggings and the boots.

Velvet skittered back to her from the balcony and climbed up her skirt to her shoulder, sniffing her damp hair. "Did you get some rest, sweetie?"

Velvet gave a cheerful chirp.

***

Kyre, dressed in gray, took her by the arm to escort her down to the cafeteria. They joined the others on the way down.

"Get some rest?" Acacia asked.

"Yes, very refreshing. And the clothes are comfy."

"No black clothing," Chloe griped. She wore an eggplant colored long dress over dark brown leggings, like Mimi. Somehow she'd managed to keep the makeup, and her eyes were rimmed in black.

Acacia just rolled her eyes. "You can wear makeup at home, but not to school."

"Yes!" Chloe fist pumped and her snoots, sitting on her shoulders, whistled. "I'm a great snoot trainer, aren't I?"

Acacia wore a medium blue flouncy dress and Hannah wore a dusty mauve one, with her long hair in a fishtail braid.

"I want braids like that," Chloe told her.

"I'll come over early tomorrow and do your hair," Hannah promised.

They met up with Grady, in a dark green tunic with the same leggings and boots the women had. Tris, Trineal and Zhuzhana joined them and they walked to the cafeteria. Kyre and Mimi shared a few secret glances.

The cafeteria was open. Tall pillars with low walls between them, planted with greenery and flowers, surrounded the space. Long tables and individual chairs filled the room. Many were full. Kyre and the other Valryssians waved and chatted with friends.

"The day after tomorrow your translator chips will begin working, and you'll get to know more people," Zhuzhana said. "I work as a medic just down the path. Come see me anytime you feel lonely."

"Your English is good," Acacia said.

Zhuzhana smiled. "The clan has a special upgrade for new members."

It turned out she and Trineal lived across the park, while Tris lived on a different level near the Bridge, in crew housing.

"I have pink glitter lights on my balcony. Can't miss it," she said cheerfully.

The meal was good, a meat portion and many vegetables and fruits. "All the produce is grown on the ship. We have two levels of garden," Kyre said. "We'll take a tour tomorrow."

After the meal, they all wandered through the park. Chloe played on the swing. Mimi and Kyre walked on the perimeter path, where they had some privacy.

When they finally went up to the sixth floor, Kyre said, "I have Jenvil wine"

The wine turned out to be in an expensive – looking cut crystal bottle. It was sweet with bubbles. They sat on his balcony swing. The residential area was now dark, with lighted paths. Balconies across the park lit up with moving, twinkling lights. Many did patterns, a few did some type of animation. Jellyfish type animals were popular.

Velvet, on her shoulder, gave a series of chirps and whistles, and other snoots answered her. She leaped away, climbed down the balcony and disappeared. "Must be going nano-hunting," Kyre whispered, and then kissed her.

Mimi placed her goblet on the table so she could kiss him properly.

***

The next days were busy. Medical checkups, translator chips upgraded. They enjoyed the tour of the huge ship. A few days after reconfiguration, the translator chips worked, and they received armbands that opened to a hologram computer screen.

A tutor named Agri, a tall older woman of the three eyed type, worked with them on tutorials to use the tiny visual interface in their eye and the holocoms. "Until you have more experience in languages, you will need to refer to the vis to see what language you are speaking. It takes time to speak the languages. You'll understand them long before you can speak well. And some issues will always remain in speaking different languages, since your soft palate is already formed for your native language."

"So we'll sound weird?" Chloe asked.

The woman smiled. "Some languages, like Bisk, will always be difficult. The Alliance Standard language is made to be easy for many people."

"Will our language be added to the database?" Acacia asked.

The woman tilted her head toward her shoulder, the way the Clan indicated no. "For now, it will remain as a Valryssian secret. It is quite helpful to have an unknown language when dealing with trade negotiations."

By keeping their tutoring schedules and assignments, they were compensated at a Level One pay grade, so they all had steles to spend at the upcoming Haven Gathering Marketplace. Level Two compensation was even better, that would happen after they were assigned a job.

Mimi had yet to spend a night in her own apartment, and she was quite happy with that.

***

They met a few days later in a conference room near the Bridge to learn about the Shen ship.

Captain Rhodes Valryssian was older than Kyre, probably mid-thirties. They had met socially at a welcoming meal, where he was accompanied by his children. His wife, a Striker flight instructor, had died in a training accident several years ago.

Now he stood in front of a view screen in a dark burgundy uniform with gold accents. Kyre, as First Officer, was also dressed in burgundy, but with gray trim, indicating senior officers and Bridge officers. Different jobs and levels of seniority wore different uniforms. Medics like Zhuzhana wore a dusty pink with light gray trim.

"We thought you would like to hear the results of the Shen slave ship investigation. Commander Mik Miline of Fera Border Patrol is here to give a report."

Mil Miline, a female wearing a dull green uniform with dark plum braid on the shoulders, stood up. She was one of the humanoids with a bony protuberance from the forehead to the end of the nose.

Everyone was speaking Standard, Mimi noticed.

"Good day. We are pleased the crew of Red Haven helped us apprehend Trade Alliance slavers. The Shen ship held a total of one hundred and eighty-two captives, to be sold at auction. They are being treated and rehomed as much as possible. Some, like yourselves, are from a homeworld that doesn't traverse interstellar space. They will be educated and assisted by Planet Fera."

"Red Haven has agreed to support and educate the five of you, plus ten more of the victims will go to other Haven ships," Captain Rhodes said.

The Commander smiled and continued. "Prince Ammoni Skev, commander of the Shen ship, is in

Alliance prison awaiting trial. The Shen Federation will be given a series of sanctions, one being the confiscation of all deep space vessels that enter Alliance Space. Their planet now has Federated Military beyond its boundaries.

"All Shen children aboard the vessel, and caregivers who were not involved in ship's operations, will be returned to Shen. The rest of the crew will be imprisoned on the Fera Asteroid Mines, assuming they receive a guilty verdict at their trials."

"The ship Shen Rick Vell will be sold at auction. One fourth of the sale will go to Fera Border Patrol, after holding fees to the space dock are paid. One fourth to the Federated Space Corps monitoring the Shen Boundaries. The rest will be divided among the victims."

Mimi's eyes nearly popped with that. Wouldn't that be a lot of steles? They had already received fifty thousand steles apiece for the Wormship, sold to a Valryssian on Doona.

That night, while Kyre was on duty, the four Earth women and Grady broke open a bottle of expensive Fera Lavender Wine and had snacks in Acacia's kitchen. All the snoots and Kyre's cat pack ended up on the balcony, where Chloe fed them snacks, too.

Their talk turned to future careers. "Security," Grady said. "I know, no surprise. I get weapons training. Eventually, I may qualify to fly a Striker, but that would be a few years away. So much to learn."

Acacia was taking the most comprehensive course of study, with the goal of being an Operation's Officer. She would learn to oversee many departments on board and have a good overview of the entire ship departments and processes. "My goal is to be a Second Officer, the Bridge Operations head."

"I'm going into financial management, which, while not a thrill a minute, is important work for the Haven. I've had all the Star Wars excitement I'll ever need," Mimi said.

Mimi expected Hannah to go into education and childcare. But Hannah surprised everyone by choosing a course of study almost as comprehensive as Acacia's. "I'm going to be an Environmental Control Technician, working on air quality, water quality, bio spaces and radiation oversight. I do want to eventually be a Greenspace tech, but I have to know all the systems, since they all have to coordinate."

"I'm impressed you chose that course of study," Mimi told her privately while Grady related a hilarious story about his latest physical training incident. "So different from your previous work."

Hannah nodded. "After the aptitude test, I had a lot to think about. All my skills pointed me into the sciences, or medicine. I had to make a decision."

She sipped her wine. "I never made the decision to be in charge of the Children's programs at the church, I just did what was expected. I liked it, but I am not creative or flexible enough for a job like that. It was always a headache."

She placed her drink down and looked at Mimi. "You know, I've never made a big decision alone before. Not like you, on your own, working and going to college. Kind of delayed development for my age, I guess. My father dictated everything, and I agreed with him. I was taught that way. Now... I miss him, but I don't miss that life very much. Now, my life is full of anticipation. I love to garden. This way, I can be involved in what I love."

"We all come from different backgrounds. My mom died, and who knows where my dad is? All I have are two elderly aunts in Arizona. So I had only myself to make decisions."

Hannah grinned. "I suspect you won't be on your own for too much longer."

CHAPTER NINE

"You have magnets in your skin, right? Some alien thing?" Mimi was draped over Kyre. "That is the only logical explanation. I'm not normally so friendly with a man I just met."

Kyre snorted. "No magnets."

Velvet, who was swinging on a small arm lamp over the bed, did a flip with much churring. "Laughing at me, are you?" She placed the snoot on the carpet. "Go find your friends."

She turned back to Kyre and waggled a finger at him. "We'll have to do a lab test. I'm human, my blood is full of iron. Your magnet skin pulls me in."

"If you say so." He pulled her close. "We have a little time before we go to the family meeting."

Kyre had fancy Fera Silk sheets on his bed. His apartment was filled with pictures and art objects he'd collected over time. Her rooms still had the stark look of a new residence. She loved his place.

Kyre pulled her close. "Mimi, when we have the Family Gathering Feast, would you like to stand up with me and declare a betrothal? It is not binding. We don't even have to share the same quarters."

"Are there legal things I should know about?"

"If we buy property, it belongs to both of us. Big property, like land, businesses, or ships. Things like clothing don't count. So, if we do not pair bond in the future, we will need to make arrangements for the shared property. Or children, if we had a them."

"I'd rather be pair bonded before having a child."

"I agree. But if we had a surprise, we could choose to pair bond or stay in a betrothal, or go separate ways except for the care of the child."

"All right. That all makes sense." She suddenly felt shy. "Um, Kyre." She took a deep breath. "What if I moved in here? I never use my apartment."

He smiled, his open, happy smile, not a polite, social one. "I would love that."

***

Months later

The Red Haven arrived at the secret location of the Gathering of the Valryssian Clan. The Earth women went up to the observatory lounge to watch the ship connect to the Gathering station. The station was a huge disk-shaped vessel with docking bays all around the perimeter. Below was long spiral arm for smaller ships. "It looks like you have a lot of ships already," Mimi said.

"I count nine of the fifteen Havens. The Blue Haven is my mother's ship. Close to forty smaller ships.. That spiral is extendable, so we can dock many small ships."

"Are the small ships all Valryssians?" Acacia asked.

"Yes, all are Clan. They might be small traders or families that have short or unusual trade routes. I will make it available for you to tour a few of those small ships, they are pretty interesting, all so different. We can also take tours of all the different Havens, though you will find them much the same as Red Haven. Some, however, have a great deal more agriculture with animals and green spaces. I enjoy visiting those."

Robotic arms guided the Red Haven was into a docking area and clamped to the station. "They'll have the passageway secure in a few minutes. Why don't you all go get a bag or whatever you need for a few hours away, and we'll meet on Deck Four."

"Tomorrow I will be in meetings all day," Kyre told Mimi as they walked back to their apartment. "But I heard that Zhuzhana is going to meet up with her sister and take you all to the marketplace. I think you will find it an enjoyable experience."

"Especially since we have money to spend," said Chloe.

Mimi thought Captain Rhodes was intimidating. That was nothing compared to Kyre's mother, Captain Quandra, who she met that evening at a private dinner. Quandra stood over six feet, her skin was teal, but instead of the dark hair of Kyre and his brothers, her hair was bright gold. She had the three eyes, from her Trengulu ancestry, but instead of the sheer, decorative scarf over her third eye, she wore a band of shiny black leather. She looked ...commanding. Her eyes searched Mimi thoroughly. Mimi willed herself not to squirm.

"You showed yourself resourceful on Grzbt."

"Thank you, Captain."

Quandra waved a long, three fingered hand. "Please, call me Ami. Soon you will be betrothed to my Kyre."

Mimi cleared her throat. "But my companions also were resourceful and full of ideas. And we had amazing luck, with the Shikshik getting squished. And the costumes."

Ami raised an eyebrow. "In my life I have had such luck. Often it is seeing an opportunity and grabbing it. Not everyone can see the opportunities before them." She waved her hand at a waiter in the restaurant. "A bottle of Crax?"

The waiter brought her a clear liquid in a carafe with tiny two cups. "Drink with me," Ami said. "I have decided you are more than worthy of my Kyre. And I am quite hard to please. I am extraordinarily happy he did not choose a reckless fighter pilot as his bride." She poured two drinks in the delicate cups, and shot hers back.

Mimi knew she was referring to Rhodes deceased wife. *Awkward*. She hurriedly slammed back the small cup. Her brain and throat froze. *Cold. Floral ice*. She dragged in a breath.

Velvet leaped off her shoulder, headed to her cup before Mimi snatched it away. *No way, Velvet*.

"Crax, Ami? Really? On first meeting? Mimi, don't go over two cups, or I will have to carry you home," Kyre said. Mimi nodded, already feeling the effects of the drink.

"I'm celebrating, my son. I like your choice. She has strong intestines and recognizes opportunities." Quandra shot back another glass. Mimi shared hers with Kyre. Quandra slammed the tiny cup onto the table and poured another drink. "I like that she is in finance."

"What color are you wearing for your Declaration?" Quandra asked, after her fourth cup of crax.

"Silver with dark purple trim."

"Delightful. I will loan you my Trengulu sapphires."

Kyre's father, Lor, was a teacher of Systems and Cultures, like a sociologist. He looked human but had copper skin, white hair and twisted horns. In contrast to his wife, he seemed friendly, even affable. "You must come to our quarters soon for an evening of games," he said.

"Wouldn't miss it, Abi," Kyre said, using the Trengulu name for father.

"Mother likes you," Kyre said as they walked to their apartment. "That makes everything so much easier."

"She seems...demanding?"

"Mother is from a warrior clan. It was quite the scandal when she married my father, a scholar. He was quite older."

The next morning the Earth women, Grady, Zhuzhana and her sister Luzhana, left to shop in the

Marketplace. Little Theless, Rhode's daughter, joined them for the excursion.

Mimi had a big plan. She had to get a worthy gift for Kyre, as it was part of the Declaration Ceremony. It had to be a treasured keepsake of beauty and value. She knew just what she wanted and had the steles in her account to buy it.

"It looks like Quandra likes you," Zhuzhana said.

"She thinks I'm resourceful. And she likes that I'm in nice, safe, finance."

Zhuzhana laughed. "She likes that I have no Valryssian blood and work in a residential clinic, fixing sprains and skinned knees. She wants many grandchildren."

The floor they came to was an enormous circular open area, filled with hundreds of booths carrying all kinds of goods. There were many fascinating things, exotic plants, furniture, clothing. Things the Earth people didn't understand like medical equipment. It had the air of a street fair with music playing, little tables set out for drinks and snacks provided by small Bots. Children ran about with balloons and face paint and the crowd made lots of noise.

"I'm looking at everything before I spend any money," Chloe said. "I'd hate to spend all my money only to find something I really, really want in the last booth. Chloe had received her share of the Wormship and the Shen ship, but Kyre and Acacia were overseers.

Acacia made sure she had a generous amount for the Gathering. "Why scrimp?" she had asked.

"Good plan. I think I'll do much the same, except I am on the lookout for a worthy gift for Kyre. I know just what I want, too," Mimi said.

Zhuzhana turned. "What are you getting him?"

"Kyre has a small shelving unit that is made of black crystal. It seems to have inner lights. So beautiful. I'd like to get him another one, hopefully much larger. He has an empty corner in his bedroom, and it would pick up the lights from the balcony twinkles."

"I know where we can inquire about specific items," Zhuzhana said. "Let me check. I know exactly what you're talking about, I've kind of wanted one of those for a while. They are very beautiful. Expensive, though."

Mimi grinned. Expensive didn't frighten her.

"Found it! Outer circle that direction." Zhuzhana waved.

They walked to a section of furniture and other household good vendors. Mimi found the black crystal dealer. Silyrian Crystal, it was called.

"Is there something I can help you with?" The blue skinned vendor asked.

"Yes, I am looking for a shelf, as large as possible," Mimi said.

"I have larger goods in the back. Please follow me."

She followed him into the back of his booth behind a divider that hid his packing crates. "I keep my larger items in their crates for easier transport for the buyer," he said. "If you find what you want, I'll have a bot deliver it to your apartment."

"Thank you." She began looking at the different shelves. There was one that was lovely, but only two feet tall. The corner could take something much large. She picked up the small shelf. Maybe she would buy it, also, for the living room.

She held it, since it wasn't heavy, and wandered to the other crates.

Velvet ran out of her pocket and up to her forearm. She began screeching. "Churr churr *eet*!"

A second later, Mimi smelled the stench. That rancid odor that could only mean one thing. There was a worm somewhere nearby.

She looked around wildly through the crowded market for a worm, but didn't see one.

Then she found the disgusting ooze trail moving to a slit in the canvas-like draping of the booth. She crept over and peered through it. There was a worm, filthy as always, holding a tube, which she knew was called a matter disruptor. The weapon was pointed directly at Hannah, who had wandered across the aisle, looking at a selection of neon colored kittens. Her back was to the worm.

Mimi screamed, "Worms!"

Startled, people moved around. The white haired kitten vendor saw the worm, grabbed Hannah and dragged her behind his table, to the floor.

Velvet leaped off her arm and ran. Mimi ran also, right behind the worm. "Oh no you don't!" She screeched.

As she yelled Mimi smacked the worm with the shelf with all her strength. It fell to the floor, but she knew that wouldn't stop it. Those worms were tough.

Suddenly, more worms oozed their way to her. She dodged to the next booth.

"Worms!" Her cry alerted the other women.

Zhuzhana and Lushana gave each other a look, and lifted the veils over their third eyes. Little Theless did the same. Mimi could see Grady, Kyre and the murder cats streaking to them while the worms lowered themselves to the floor and snaked through the merchandise.

The Trengulu women open their third eyes and beams of sharp white light came out, boring straight through the worms. Little Theless had a softer light, but it still caused damage, making the worms smoke and screech.

Mimi ran back to the large crates to hide, still clutching the small but beautiful shelf. Hidden, she watched at the commotion but took a moment to peek inside the crate.

The Holy Grail of shelves.

Kyre, Grady and the cats soon had the worms wrapped in something sticky. "Congratulations ladies, you did good work today. I think we'll have to give you a commendation." He grinned at Theless. "Or maybe a toy."

A narrow, bullet shaped vehicle sped down the path toward them. Several guards rode it like a horse, but Captain Quandra, in a shiny, formfitting black suit with blue trim and with shiny silver spirals, stood upright, golden hair flowing behind, as it hurtled toward the scene.

Mimi ran to Kyre, who hugged her tight. The white-haired kitten vendor, his arm around Hannah as if she was a most tender flower, came up next to them.

Queen Boadicea of Space leaped off the transport. "Who dares to harm the Valryssian clan?" Quandra roared.

The white-haired guy who was petting Hannah's hair, leaned over toward Kyre. "Crax?"

"You know it. Always scarier with Crax."

Kyre turned to Mimi. "Mimi, this is my cousin Valnor Valryssian from Doona. Valnor, this is Hannah and Mimi, who I will Declare with at the Feast. They are two of the Earth women."

"Lovely to meet you," Valnor said, not taking his golden eyes off Hannah.

Kyre hugged Mimi. "Are you all right?"

"I'm fine. The worm was actually pointing his tube at Hannah when I first saw it, and then all the other ones came up from behind me. They must have been in the packing crates."

He pressed soft kisses on her head.

"Thank goodness Zhuzhana, Lushana, and Theless could use their third eye. I'm afraid we would have gotten kidnapped for a third time, which is damned hard to believe." She knew she was babbling in relief.

Hannah still looked shocked. She leaned against the well-built kitten vendor and clutched his arm.

Quandra finished her investigation of the scene.

"Kyre, you should take your young lady to the Starlight. Hot water and bubbly drinks are what these young women need. And you, Valnor, where are your manners? Get that young woman to the Starlight."

"Yes, Aunt Quandra." Valnor went to close his booth. "Hannah, do you want one? My treat. We can take it with us, night hunters love hot water."

Hannah was stunned out of her shock. "The yellow one?"

He popped the butter yellow kitten into a carry cage, added a sack of supplies, and took her arm.

Mimi watched, wide-eyed.

"Are these murder cats? I mean Night Hunter cats?" Chloe asked Valnor.

"Yes, want one? These are miniatures neons."

"Sure, I can pay."

"You keep your money. I'm not actually a trader."

"Oh? What do you do?" Hannah asked while Chloe picked out a neon pink kitten. Chloe's nanosnoots came out from her belt to meet the kitten.

"Oh, I developed the latest hull. Kittens are a hobby."

"Ready?" Kyre asked.

"No. I have one thing to do." She sprinted to the crystal booth.

"Grady, I saw how you reacted. Good man. I'll be keeping an eye on you. Please escort the sisters and my little granddaughter to the Starlight. Buy Theless a toy. On my steles, of course." Quandra tossed a small bag to Grady.

Grady snagged it, grinned, and took Lushana by the elbow. Theless gave her grandmother a hug and then ran off shouting. "I know what I want!"

Mimi finished her purchase and joined Chloe, Hannah and Acacia. Finally, they all strolled to the Starlight, a restaurant that featured a shallow hot pool with a tables for drinks and snack. The lighting was dim with many colored twinkle lights.

"Romantic," Mimi whispered to Kyre.

A type of loose tunic was provided to wear in the water, and Zhuzhana ordered fancy drinks and snacks for everyone.

"This is relaxing," Acacia said. "I still want to shop, though."

"Me, too," Mimi said, leaning back against Kyre. "I have to check on our Declaration clothes."

"I think I'll go home and try some shopping later this week. I have to help Daffodil settle in," Hannah said, hovering over the swimming kitten. She was sitting with Valnor, who was holding her arm close.

"Somehow, I don't think Lushana and my brother-in-law are going to declare," Zhuzhana said, glancing over her shoulder. Grady and Lushana were sitting close together, talking, away from the group. And something might be happening, there."

She flicked a glance at Hannah and Valnor, who were staring into each other's eyes.

"God above," Acacia said. "Something must be in the air." She scooted closer to Mimi. "Chloe, come sit next to me. I do not want to meet the alien of my dreams right now." Chloe giggled but she sat next to Acacia.

After snacking next to Acacia for a while, Chloe and her kitten had attracted a group of children and she and Theless left to have fun in a kiddie area.

"At least I got my worthy gift purchased," Mimi said. "From the stress of spaceworms to the stress of a formal social function."

"I know which one I'd rather have," Hannah said.

Mimi grinned at her.

***

The Feast was on the last evening of the Gathering. Mimi had learned that Kyre's family were the direct descendants of Wilhelm the super genius, and a Trengulu woman named Shaundra Valryssian. From this family line other geniuses, one a generation, were born. It made them close to royalty among trading clans.

The current super genius was Valnor, who both developed the advanced hull technology, and, for some reason, changed all the plant life of his continent to shades of purple. He raised different breed of Night Hunters as a hobby.

"Valryssian super geniuses are unpredictable," Kyre told her.

Mimi inspected herself. Hannah had done her almost shoulder-length hair into a crown of fancy loose braids. The silver gown was sheer silver flounces, embroidered in eggplant scroll work, sleeveless with thin straps. The sapphires from Quandra, bright purple teardrops interspersed with diamonds, were perfect. Worth a fortune, she was sure.

She liked how she looked. Hopefully she wouldn't be so nervous it spoiled the ceremony.

Kyre met her in the living room. He looked handsome in silver gray with eggplant embroidery.

"Ready for this?"

Ready for life with Kyre, in space as part of trading clan? Velvet climbed up her flounces and chirped softly in her ear.

She took his arm. "Can't wait."

The End

TERMS AND NAMES

Places:

Fera: resort planet
Grzbt: Commercial space station
Doona: planet belonging to the Valryssians
Red Haven, Haven: Large, city sized trader spaceship

Peoples:

Trengulu: humanoid, blue skin tone. Females have the third laser eye
Telenn, rather human-like but with white crystalline skin and hair. White or light blue eyes. Males have two horns
Bisk: bird type alien race
Kulag: Elephant nose humanoids, with large long-lashed eyes.
Shikshik: worm aliens

Aliarietts: Chloe's 'Dobbys'. Tiny, thin, floppy ears

Shen: Bronze skin, some with horns, white or blond hair. *Shen Rick Vell*: slaver ship

Characters:

The Valryssian Family: surname, clan name, have an Earth ancestor. Wealthy, powerful traders
Kyre, First Officer, Red Haven
Captain Rhodes, Red Haven, Kyre's oldest brother, widower
Rhodes's children: Galileo, Cassien and Theless Valryssian, half Trengulu
Tris and Trineal Valryssian, Techs, Kyre's younger twin brothers
Trineal's bride Zhuzhana, a medic
Lushana, Zhuzhana's sister.
Alyxin, Zaver, and Strongbow(part Kulag): cousins and security guards
Grady McCall, abducted Marine rescued from slave ship
Quandra, Captain of Blue Haven, Trengulu, their mother
Lor, their father, a sociology professor. Earth ancestry.
Valnor , super genius cousin from Doona
Agri, tutor
Wilhelm Heinz: Great-grandfather from Earth. Super genius escaped the Third Reich, made it to space in a homemade ship. Rescued by Trengulu traders.

Animals:
Murder Cats: Mitsy, Mother of Slayers, Eenie, Meenie, Miney, Moe

Velvet: Nanosnoot: small elephant-nosed mousy lab creation

Terms:
Annums: years
Steles: cube money
 Silyrian Crystal- black crystal with an inner glow.
Tube path: A Space elevator

ABOUT THE AUTHOR

Bio

Take a bookworm. Hand her a stack of her much older brother's Sci-fi and fantasy novels, thrillers and horror comics. Then introduce the world of romance.

Make her a jinx. Every great genre TV show she loves gets the ax! So often the romances have no happy ending. She gets upset about no romance in the world and writes her own stories with happy endings.

Throw this all together, shake constantly, and pour onto a computer keyboard.

There!

You have me,

Melisse Aires

I have a newsletter!
https://sendfox.com/melisseaires

Join the fun Scifi Romance Group and also Romancing the Shire on Facebook.

Please review if you enjoyed this romance!

Facebook:
https://www.facebook.com/melisseaires

Blog: https://http://melisseaires.blogspot.com/

Website/Newsletter:
http://www.melisseairesbooks.com
Twitter: https://twitter.com/Melisse_Aires
Facebook:
https://www.facebook.com/melisseaires
IO News Group:
https://groups.io/g/MelisseAiresPureEscapism